SEAN M. T. SHANAHAN

As Darkness Falls,
The Hunters Become The Prey

THE DAUGHTER OF DARKNESS

PART I

DRAGON WRATH

One war had ended—or so people thought—and now the real war would begin. The true enemy pressed in on many fronts, from above and below, and there were few in this world who could contend with the true nature of the threat.

The Dragon watched from its peak as the sun crept over the edge of the world. It shifted wings and scales to dislodge the night's frost, which drifted away in the gales. As the sun dispelled the night, souls in their thousands were released from their ghoulish hosts. They sailed away from the islands upon the water, their passage unseen to most eyes but his.

The War of the Damned had ended, but soon people would come to realise it was but a mere skirmish in the machinations of evil.

Many of those freed souls would not make it to paradise . . .

The Dragon watched their path, an aurora of green soul stuff surging into the dying of the night sky.

There was another battle raging between the stars. The souls would find their path was not safe, but others would fight that battle. It was not the Dragon's place to intervene.

No.

It was not its place at all.

Things were changing, oaths had been forsaken, guardians had been scattered, and soon the foundations of the world itself would shift and shatter. Maybe the Dragon had no place anymore, and maybe that meant it *could* act . . .

It felt it even now, the weakened veils of this plane withering away; the unwitting vanguard of the true threat gnawing its way into this reality. There were some fonts of strength left to repel them, but they would soon be unguarded. The enemy would converge upon these places—their defencelessness shining like a beacon—and surge through to this world en masse.

Perhaps it *was* time the Dragon became involved? The natural order was being undone, after all. Either way, after a thousand years it sensed it would soon be time to join the voyage of souls, and its safe passage was now no longer guaranteed. Fear, a fleeting pinch of something not felt in an age . . . The Dragon snorted. A wisp of smoke curled from its nostrils before the mountain wind tore it away.

That settled it then.

The Dragon reared and spread its wings; they caught the gale as its amber scales reflected the sunlight, and it lifted from its perch upon the peak.

The veils had already been breached, and there was but one thing left to do.

With a titanic whump the Dragon launched forward and flattened its wings against its hide. It dived away from the sun, back into the shadow of the mountain where night still lingered. It skimmed the sloping surface as it descended with the fury of a hailstorm. Wind and ice whistled past its serpentine features, melting from the sheer heat the Dragon exuded and splattering across the white slopes as condensed mist.

The roots of the mountain rushed to slam into the Dragon, and with a hurricane it splayed its wings again. The forests that clustered at the mountain's base bent as if struck by a great force. Leaf and critter and shrub launched into the air to fill the vacuum created by the membranes of the beast. With another whump the

Dragon launched itself over the forests and tore across brightening skies towards a wooded glen.

Despite being some leagues away, the Dragon's flight was so fast, the glen approached within moments.

It circled the little glen in the dark, scouting for the font. From its vantage point, firelight from several villages winked like weak stars against the dim woods, and the Dragon closed its eyes in sorrow.

There was nothing else to do; it had a duty to perform. It could already sense the vanguard of the true threat breaking through the undefended points in this realm to converge on this spot.

With a heavy heart the Dragon inhaled, summoning fire into its belly. It flattened its wings and dived again, making a beeline for the village closest to the centre of the glen. The Dragon was not sure the villagers would see it approach, but it was sure they would see the destruction it left. The Dragon exhaled, amber flame searing a swathe of the forest leading towards the village.

After gouging a trail of fire in the woods so thick that several wagons could traverse it side by side, the village warning bell rang.

The Dragon banked around the village and breathed another swathe of fire into the woods as the poor denizens spilled out of their homes and the palisade gates, fleeing to the next town to warn them of the danger.

There was nothing they could do to stop it—the Dragon knew. It continued its path of destruction, carving a circle of fire into the glen so large that none could mistake its intent. *This territory is mine now. Cross this line and burn.*

It circled its new little spot deep within the wooded glen and finally came to land upon a knoll with a bubbling stream that spewed from its top. The different paths of flowing water parted around deeply carved druid stones . . . This was the place.

Now the Dragon would stand guard, and it hoped its fellow kind would do the same at the other strongholds of this plane. It was not sure a Dragon *could* stand against the might of what was coming, but there were few other beings that could stand in contest against it. The necromancers were gone, their tasks forsaken, and the plane was fracturing for it. Soon, the enemy would be here. The Dragon waited, knowing that it would not only have to contend with the enemy, but with the misguided attempts by the locals to drive it off. It would also have to do battle with heroes . . .

PART II

WAYWARD HEROES

The noose was pulled tight around the magistrate's neck, the rope burning his skin with the friction as he suppressed the urge to swallow.

"Now you know I'm serious!" Commander Crauld shouted up at the gallows in the town square.

The magistrate couldn't help but smirk, eyeing the corpse of the poor messenger next to him as it swayed in the breeze. It was actually a lovely day, all things considered. The sun was shining in the late morning, the sky was pristine blue, and there was a crisp breeze from the mountains that possessed a hint of woodsmoke. The townspeople were being cajoled into the square by dishevelled soldiers who barked angrily. Deserters, all of them, they acted the tough oppressor, but their expressions were stricken. That made the magistrate smirk too, in a sad sort of way.

"Are you even listening, man?" Crauld shrieked. "You're about to be hung!"

Hanged, the magistrate hissed internally. *You troglodyte.* "That much is obvious, Commander. What isn't obvious is how you'd like me to respond to that information?"

Crauld gasped in frustration, looking at his second in command—a stony-faced troll who shrugged in confusion. "I *want* you to sign this document," he waved a crumpled scroll in the magistrate's direction, "and officialise the fact that you invited my regiment to occupy this town in order to defend it from waves of the damned. There's a haunted burial ground nearby; it isn't *that* much of a stretch!"

The magistrate chuckled even though the rope still burned against his throat. "It seems you failed, Commander. *I* am damned by the looks of it, and I've been here the whole time!" His laugh rasped across the square, the barking soldiers and mumbling townspeople stopping to watch in abject shock.

"Stop laughing!" Crauld stamped his foot.

"But it's so funny!" the magistrate said. "You desert your post and occupy a quiet town, seeking to live the rest of your miserable lives in carnal pleasure before the dead drag you into their ranks. You pillaged our stores, coerced our men and women into your beds, and drank our ale until your guts ran down our gutters . . . and then, a poor messenger strolls in. He informs you that the world will not end, that the necromancers have been defeated, and the War of the Damned is over! With his honest work he holds a mirror up to your face and to the faces of your soldiers, and you see that you are cowards, that better people did your duty where you quailed and ran. And the funniest thing is that the one man who can save you from the reckoning of the living is the one man you now have strung up to die!"

"But you won't die!" Crauld shrieked. "Sign this document and no one has to die!"

"Oh come now, Commander. We both know that I am a dead man. You can't risk me reporting this to anyone. You can't risk anyone here telling the truth. As soon as I ratify your presence here, we are as damned as your own soul."

Crauld squirmed. "I can make it hurt," he whispered.

"I'm sure you can."

"I can make them all suffer."

"I'm sure you will. But ultimately, you and your fellow deserters will be hunted, tried, and executed in a manner fitting of scum. I have known deserters in my time whom I supported. I have known traitors with some shred of honour, and warlords with competence. My only regret is that I am not to die by their hands, but at the hands of a wretch!"

Crauld's face hardened, his ears flushing red. "Gorgen." His troll lieutenant stood to attention. "Round up the children first."

Gorgen turned and barked orders to the other soldiers, who started prying the children away from their families. The families rioted in response but were struck back easily as all the fighting men and women were called away to the War of the Damned. The magistrate watched the horrid scene unfold with a heavy heart, knowing that they were all going to be killed anyway, and they were likely going to be killed in *sporting* ways. Both for the amusement of the animals who once called themselves soldiers, and so that it seemed this town was raided by bandits or the dead before they were halted at the Dwarf Islands. He sighed. *Such is life . . .*

As the children were huddled into the town centre and the old and weak were kept at bay, Crauld turned back to the magistrate once more.

"I can have my warlock burn them into crisps. This is your last chance, Magistrate. Fulfil your duty, protect your people."

The magistrate chuckled again, but this time there was venom in his voice. "How dare you."

"Very well!" Crauld barked. "Gorgen, get Kullyn to . . ." He was interrupted by a voice.

"Alms!" It was a deep voice, loud, raspy, and accompanied by a rattle of coin.

The gathered turned from the magistrate and down the main road, which was lined with two-storied buildings of grey brick and wooden slat. A dwarf in raggedy grey robes hobbled down the street with a stooped gait, rattling a rusty flagon in one hand that jingled as he chanted his plea.

"Alms, alms, alms for the poor. Alms for the refugees in this war. Alms, alms, alms for the poor . . ." He was halted by a spindly orc at the edge of the crowd.

"Gorgen," Crauld hissed, "why did the guards not stop that person from entering the town?"

"Because your people are incompetent," the magistrate said quietly, but he looked down the main road in wonder himself. The gates listed open, manned on either side by two guards who stood to what he would describe as inattention. Beyond the gates was a wagon being slowly pulled towards the town by two taller people in rags as destitute as the dwarf's—the magistrate assumed they were human.

"It's just a beggar," Gorgen grumbled. "I suppose they didn't think it mattered."

"Gorgen, if you don't get up there and flog those guards right now, I will have you flogged for their incompetence!"

"Yessir!" Gorgen saluted and pushed through the crowds towards the road.

A squadron of soldiers surrounded the dwarf beggar and menaced him with their weapons. "You're not going to find no alms here, little runt." The orc kicked the dwarf's flagon out of his hands, and three copper coins spilled out across the dirt road.

"You'll find no nothing!" A human woman stepped in to smack the dwarf across the head with the butt of her spear, and then gasped.

With enough speed to create a rush of air, the dwarf raised his hand and blocked the spear butt with a *crack*. "No alms?" He peeked up from his raggedy hood and flashed a cheeky grin, showing a solid row of tombstone-like teeth that shone through a silver beard. "How about . . . arms?" He gripped onto the spear butt, the sleeve of his robe slipping back to reveal brass gauntlets that glinted in the sunlight. With a twist the dwarf snapped the spear butt in half. He then sprang forward, slamming his gauntlet into the jaw of the hapless human. She sprawled across the ground.

Chunks of broken teeth scattered across the dirt as the dwarf murmured a deep chant, summoning spiritual amber fire around his gauntlets. He spun and struck the orc next with a hook punch to the knee. Cartilage cracked, skin burned, and sinew tore as the knee joint twisted in a way that it was not supposed to, and the orc collapsed howling.

Before the other soldiers could react, the wagon being pulled towards the town crumbled outwards. A hulking pink creature with enormous, gnarled antlers and a mighty wooden club burst out of its hiding place. It roared and charged towards the gates as the once sheepish guards struggled to close it.

The gates slammed shut when the hulking creature was mere paces away, and a guard hefted the beam in place. Before he could lock the beam to the gate, a lance of light pierced through the crack in the middle. The beams were seared in half, and a burning hole tore through the guard. He was dead before he hit the ground. And then the gates burst open.

The hulking creature broke through the gates with ease, and as it bellowed a deep war cry, the magistrate recognised it as an ogre. The two other figures who had been hauling the cart spirited through on either side of their roaring companion and discarded their robes.

One was a human man covered head to toe in steel plate armour and wielding an intricate glaive, which he used to cut down the other gate guard. The other was an elf man, with rosy skin, a white tabard, and gold-trimmed pauldrons, marking him as a paladin. The elf summoned the light of paladism into his hands and blasted the archer on the watchtower who was fumbling to nock an arrow.

"To arms!" Crauld bellowed, shuffling back behind the gallows. "I said to arms, you fools!"

The magistrate watched in fascination as the four newcomers laid about the deserters. . . Scratch that, there were five. There was a gnome scurrying between the legs of the rampaging ogre, drawing arcane runes in the air to shoot fire and lightning at the scrambling soldiers.

The attacking squadron had a game plan, that much was certain. The ogre roared and charged down the main road towards the town square. It lowered its antlers to gore the soldiers foolish enough not to scramble out of the way. Alongside of him the human warrior surged down a row of storefronts. Blade and arrow glanced off his plate armour as he expertly handled his glaive to parry and cleave at will. On the other side of the rampaging ogre's path, the elf paladin struck out with lances of holy sun fire.

The dwarf in the centre by the crowds was becoming overwhelmed as he brawled with the soldiers. But they were being picked off, whether from bolts of power from the gnome, who was dashing closer, or from arrows that whistled from some unseen archer on the rooftops.

The deserting regiment's warlock—Kullyn, a young, spindly satyr with patchy fur—stepped forward and made to strike the dwarf down with a stream of green fire. But the dwarf smashed his gauntlets together, forming a guard over his face, and chanted. He summoned a shield of spiritual fire which formed an orb around him. The green fire engulfed the amber energy and dissipated harmlessly behind the dwarf's defensive posture. The warlock started to cast another spell, but the gnome leaped through the smoke and cast a bolt of lightning.

The warlock deflected the lightning with the palm of his hand, but was on the back hoof. He turned and ran with a bleated shout. And the other nearby soldiers routed with him as they ducked into the tavern by the main square and barred the doors shut.

The dwarf and gnome pursued the routed band of soldiers as the ogre, human, and elf reached the town centre. The crowds had the sense to scatter and hide in the alleys and side streets. But the soldiers, once trained and disciplined but now turned cowards from their actions, failed to respond as a unit to the three warriors, who charged in with wrath.

"Wuppet!" The gnome lanced the tavern with bolts of lightning, each deflected by an ephemeral barrier that shimmered with violet polyps. "We need a physical attack plan here. That warlock has a magic shield."

"No shit, Gomlon!" The dwarf pulled an inky vial from his belt and lobbed it at the tavern window. The window shattered and the vial exploded, filling the tavern with blue smoke. "Once the smoke spreads past the magic shield, light it!"

"What kind of smoke was that?" Gomlon asked, dodging a stray arrow that flew from the clouded tavern window.

"It's an inflammable concoction," Wuppet replied.

"*In*-flammable? I need one that's flammable!" Gomlon jeered.

"Just light the bloody smoke!" Wuppet growled.

Gomlon grinned wickedly and cast a bolt of lightning into a tendril of blue smoke that curled out from the tavern. It lit up with a whoosh, and the fire spread along the cloud of smoke, quickly surging through the tavern. There was a pained cry from the soldiers and the warlock who had taken refuge within the shop, and the doors and windows blew open. But as quickly as it began, the fire died, replaced by thick black smoke.

"Good stuff." Wuppet cracked his brass gauntlet knuckles and turned back to the rest of the fray. "Myrrel's having fun." He gestured to the human in plate armour who had deliberately allowed a group of soldiers to encircle him.

Myrrel expertly dashed and spun, blocking and attacking simultaneously. An arrow sailed from a nearby rooftop and struck down a soldier advancing on Myrrel's back, and in response the warrior cursed. "Don't interfere, Prahtan!" he roared to the rooftops, before slamming his glaive through a rounded shield, splintering it and disarming—literally—the dwarf who was holding it.

The ogre swung his club in a wide arc and took out a trio of soldiers who were rushing him as one, foolishly hoping that numbers would aid their attack, but to no avail. The elf slid under the ogre's backswing and blinded a goblin who was scurrying beneath the recent attackers' feet. The ogre lumbered in and crushed the goblin beneath his tree trunk-like leg.

"Thank you, little elf," the ogre rumbled.

"Anytime, Ot," the elf grunted, his brow glistening with beads of sweat. "Where's the target?"

The ogre scanned the thinning battlefield, past the gallows where the magistrate waited calmly, and sighted the retreating form of the commander. "He is too far for me, Trestam."

Trestam sighed and wiped his brow. "And I am too tired to lance him. Prahtan! The target is escaping!"

There was the telltale twang of two arrows being loosed, and two more soldiers went down who were fleeing from the elf and ogre. The arrows originated from a rooftop on the side of the square, and the magistrate squinted to see who had loosed them. A figure dashed across the gaps in the roofs and scrambled to an edge before leaping into the square.

She was an orc, carrying a bow in one hand and an axe in the other; her long black hair flew behind her as she fell, her lightly scaled yellow skin reflecting the late morning sun. She hit the ground and rolled, coming up and whipping down a fleeing enemy with her bow. She discarded it, the quiver at her side now empty, and moved through two more soldiers. She used her axe like a delicate blade to evade their guard, before using it as a butchering instrument on their exposed limbs.

She made to dash around the gallows but was stopped by Gorgen the troll. She snarled and leaped up the troll, smashing into his face with her axe, which only managed to chip away flecks of his stone-like skin. The troll grabbed her by the legs and slammed her down onto the pavers with a roar.

Gorgen raised a great war hammer and made to crush her, but Ot was there in a flash. With a mighty swing from his club, the ogre walloped Gorgen in the side of the head. The troll's outer skin exploded in a hail of stone shards, while his squished brain splattered everywhere.

"Thank you, Ot," Prahtan coughed through her winded state and leaped onto her feet, taking off after Crauld, who had dashed out of the far side of the town and was heading for the woods.

"She won't catch him," the magistrate warned. "He was an incompetent soldier, but he is a fast man."

Wuppet laughed as he downed a final guard who had not the sense to surrender. "And our Prahtan is the best huntress I've ever seen. That commander had a better chance of escaping if he was strung up beside you!"

⸺••••••⸺ ⸺ ⸺••••••⸺

Prahtan sped out of the gates and hissed to herself when she saw a glint of armour disappear into the brush. She wasn't frustrated that Crauld had made it to the woods. She was frustrated that he . . .

A sudden cry cut her thoughts short.

She dashed into the brush after her quarry, finding him sprawled on the forest floor with a broken leg. He had been caught in a trapper's snare, his sword had tumbled out of his grasp, and he lay writhing in pain.

"Commander Crauld?" she asked, stepping around him as beams of sunlight shone through the forest canopy.

"Yes!" he bellowed. "How did you rig this place for traps? I had men foraging here this very morning!"

Prahtan chuckled. "I suspect you're caught in one of your own men's traps. I am actually shocked you were snared by something so . . . shoddy. I was also worried I wouldn't catch up to you before you fumbled into the old burial grounds a little way over yonder." She gestured with a nod. "Without the necromancers to do their job, the old gravesites are crawling with phantoms nowadays, and I can't claim a bounty without a body."

"There's a bounty on me?"

"You deserted your post. With a whole regiment . . . How many of your comrades fell on the front who might still be alive today if they had the support they expected from you?"

"Okay!" Crauld groaned. "Just please get me out of here. I'm in pain!"

"Like the townsfolk you terrorised?" Prahtan cocked her head. "Like that poor messenger boy you strung up? What was his crime, I wonder?"

"He was spreading word of the end of the War of the Damned. He would have reported our crimes here! I needed time to get the magistrate to sign a request to occupy the town or all of my soldiers would be executed! I was doing the right thing for my people!"

"How noble . . . I'm sure the townsfolk sympathise with you . . . Commander."

"Just please, get me out of here. You'll have your bounty, and I'll get a few more days of life."

Prahtan considered his request for a moment. She had watched him threaten the magistrate from the rooftops, and she had clenched her jaw as he ordered the children rounded up in the square. "I actually don't need your body." Prahtan readied her axe and strode towards the trapped Crauld. "Not all of it, anyway."

<hr />

Prahtan stalked back into the town square with a dripping crimson sack in one hand and a freshly cleaned axe hooked to her belt. It was around noon by now, and the sun shone into the open space, glaring off the grey pavers and spatters of blood.

Myrrel was marching up and down a row of captured deserters on their knees. Their heads were bowed, and if he was any other human, Prahtan would have assumed he was about to execute them. But, knowing Myrrel, he was likely scolding them for their errors in battle.

Gomlon sat on a bench to one side of them, her arms crossed as she tried not to snigger at Myrrel's professional ranting. Trestam—Prahtan was not surprised—was already tending to the wounded, using the holy light of paladism granted to him by the

Sun Guardians, to heal the wounded townsfolk. His shoulders were drooping, and sweat ran from his skin as if he had just run through a downpour. He had to stop soon, or he would faint.

She didn't see Wuppet at first, but as she made her way past the gallows, she saw his stocky figure down a side street. He was dealing with several elderly men outside a row of storefronts—butchers, bakers, herbalists—and handing out coins, issuing rushed instructions. Prahtan bared her short tusks in a smile.

"He's doing it again," Ot rumbled. The ogre sat on his haunches in front of the gallows, leaning on his club.

"Whatever do you mean, sweet Ot?" Prahtan threw the bloody sack on the ground, and it rolled with an accompanying crack and squelch.

"He's paying what merchants there are left in this town to give their wares to the people. He leaves himself only enough to eat a pauper's meal and restock the ingredients for his vials. He works much but has naught to show for it." Ot huffed in concern.

"He's a monk, sweet Ot." Prahtan went to his side and pressed her hands on a small gash across his forearm. "Asking him to keep his coin for himself would be like telling the sun to stop shining."

"I just wish he would stop pretending to be so hard done by all the time."

Prahtan chuckled. "What do you think his excuse will be this time?"

"Drink." Ot grinned. "I'll bet you three gold pieces he comes over with a flagon full of water."

"I bet you three pieces that I can coerce him into letting me take a drink." Prahtan winked up at Ot.

Ot pondered for a moment, then held up his meaty hand and counted off on his stubby fingers. His club was left to list and lean against his shoulder. "So that would make . . ." His brow furrowed.

"Fret less, sweet Ot." Prahtan nudged Ot playfully. "I suspect by the end of this encounter, you'll be six pieces richer than I."

Ot was still looking at his hand; then he held up his other hand and mumbled his numbers to himself . . . After a moment, his grin returned. "I bet you three gold pieces that I end up six gold pieces richer by the end of this."

"Uh, uh, uh!" Prahtan danced back and waggled her finger. "Because then you'd get an extra three pieces, making you *nine* pieces richer, meaning you'll owe me three pieces . . . making me owe you . . . Damn."

"Heh," Ot's chest rumbled with a laugh, "I don't know what you're saying, little orc, but I know you don't know either."

Prahtan laughed with him.

"Well, I'm glad someone's having a good time!" Myrrel marched over with a clanking of steel greaves; Gomlon was trotting along in his wake. "Prahtan, you promised me a challenge. These people were amateurs, less than amateurs! Do you know where the most experienced fighter from that lot got their training?" He gestured to the row of prisoners who were now under the watchful eye of a few older men Trestam had healed. "He said his old man used to beat him . . . THAT was his fighting experience! Why do you take us on these errands, Prahtan? We had a whole WAR over that way!" He pointed a steel finger north . . . Prahtan subtly looked east, where the War had just ended. "A war against literal legions of the undead! Yet we go after pretend warlords!"

"If we fought the necromancers like many of our *colleagues*, then all of the other evils of the world would have gone unchecked. Like this man." Prahtan kicked the sack with Crauld's head in it. "Wanted for deserting a coastal garrison before the necromancer Junla overran it. It was feared he was raiding the countryside as the military was occupied, and the local watches would have been too depleted from bolstering the regular forces. We stopped him, Myrrel. And for our good deeds, we'll get paid."

"Actually," Gomlon had pulled out a nail file to occupy herself while Myrrel and Prahtan argued, "the townspeople said that the deserters sacked the magistrate's treasury. If we wanna get paid, we're gonna have ta hoof it to the nearest town before that head starts to rot."

The magistrate cleared his throat as best he could. "Actually . . ." the party of heroes looked up at him on the gallows, ". . . after robbing the treasury, the soldiers decided the only safe place to keep the coin was in the safe . . . at the treasury office . . . I can pay you today for your services."

"Why is he still strung up?" Prahtan massaged her brow as Gomlon scurried up Ot's body and clambered onto his antlers to cut at the noose around the magistrate's neck. "I'm so sorry, sir. I work with idiots!"

"Oh no, please don't worry," the magistrate said as Gomlon cut the rope and then his bound wrists before climbing off Ot. Now freed, the magistrate hopped down from the block he was balancing on and massaged his neck. "Your people were quite occupied." He gave Ot a sideways look; the ogre was watching a butterfly that frolicked between his antlers. "Anyway, I can pay the bounty within the hour."

"Good!" Wuppet stumbled across to them from the side of the square, a flagon sloshing in the dwarf's hands. "I need more coin after drinking all of mine away!"

Prahtan eyed Ot, but he was still occupied with the butterfly.

"Why do you do this, Wuppet?" Trestam limped over and sat on the ground to lean up against Ot's side. "We all know you gave your money away to these poor people."

"Pfft!" Wuppet turned away and swigged from his flagon.

Prahtan's nostrils flared, scenting the liquid within it, and she smiled. "Can I have a swig of your apple juice, Wuppet?"

"Shut up!" Wuppet stormed away from the group.

"Why *does* he do it?" the magistrate asked tentatively.

But not tentatively enough. Wuppet turned and stormed right up to the magistrate, gazing up at him with a fierce expression. "'Cause who's gonna fear a dwarf monk who gives all of his coin away to the little kiddies in need, hmm? I didn't ask to become a monk! Dwarfs are supposed to be headstrong and single-minded, not all stoic and meditative! I was raised in a monastery on a mountain, which is, yes, why I talk all proper like one of you fancy pants humans! I didn't even know I was a dwarf until I was a teenager!"

"Really?" the magistrate said in shock.

"No, you fool! Of course I knew I was a dwarf! I just don't want to go around showcasing my charity because. It. Is. None. Of. Your. Business!" He pressed his finger into the magistrate with every word and then stormed off for good.

"He means well," Prahtan smiled, "but we really would like that bounty so we can move on."

"Yes, of course!" The magistrate straightened and shuffled away from the group.

Myrrel spat on the ground and stalked away too, to berate the deserters once more.

"I suppose," Trestam said, watching Myrrel march up and down the line of prisoners again, "that with this next payment you would have enough coin soon to open that hunting lodge you always wanted to? You'll be able to settle down and let Ot run the tavern while you teach people how to fend for themselves in the wilds?"

"I've had enough coin to open a hunting lodge twice over by now, Trestam."

"I know."

"I just . . ." Prahtan sighed. "Ot's hearts are too wild to settle down behind a bar. And I need more than that right now too. I know I'll need more than that; I'm just not sure what that means. And besides," she looked at him, "we help people doing this. We make a difference to people who had no hope."

"And so long as you intend to help people, I shall follow you," Trestam said with a weary smile. "The world will soon need many more parties like us, I fear."

"Well, Myrrel needs more than that, *now*," Gomlon said, leaning up against the gallows. "He's fed up with deserters and raiders who were too soft to venture into the war-torn lands . . . We need a greater challenge, Prahtan. The warlock attached to this regiment was a child playing at magic, and the fighters were nothing more than brawlers. Myrrel needs more and I need more."

"Be careful what you wish for," Ot rumbled.

At that, there was a dull tone from the bell on the watchtower. One of the townsfolk was put on lookout by the gate shortly after the town was liberated.

Prahtan sighed and went about gathering arrows to refill her quiver before Trestam stilled her preparations. "Fret not, huntress. It is a messenger."

"Thank the gods," Prahtan said. "If it was another subpar foe, then Myrrel would have chucked a fit."

A few moments later an elf trotted through the gates and dashed down the main road. He was light on his feet but looked weary from days of running. He wore sturdy leather armour and reeked of smoke and was covered in dirt and charcoal. He skittered to a halt before the party who stood ready at the gallows, his eyes drifting to the other messenger, who was only just now being lowered down by the townsfolk.

"Peace, brother." Trestam approached the runner with outstretched palms. "We have liberated this town from bandits recently. What news do you bring?"

The messenger was panting but stoic. He looked from the body of the other messenger, to Trestam, to Ot, Prahtan, the rest of the party, and back to Trestam. "Dragon," he blubbered, his emotions finally broiling over as he collapsed to his knees. "A dragon has attacked the villages in the nearby glen and has created a lair somewhere within the forest. It has destroyed two towns . . . A bounty has been approved by the local governor."

"What is the bounty?" Prahtan strode forward, but no matter what it was, she already knew she was going to take the job.

"The weight of its head in gold." The messenger composed himself. "Forgive me, I ran from my village as it burned, straight to the nearest city to get this approved. I've been running for two days straight since then spreading the news, but you are among the first party I have seen who might be up to the task."

"Might?" Myrrel stepped forward.

"I mean no offense, warrior." The messenger bowed. "We believe this is the dragon from White Sun Peak. It is older than even I and astonishingly devastating."

"No offense taken. I need a challenge, and if this dragon is as fearsome as you say . . ." Myrrel eyed Prahtan, who nodded.

"We shall take on this quest," she said, and then she turned to her party. "Are you ready for another hunt?"

PART III

THE STRANGER

The air hung still over the brush like the silence after a storm—but the storm had not even begun.

Laylen fled through the tangled thorns, and the creature hunting her drew closer. Catching brambles brought bleeding blight from her soft features as she tore through the undergrowth and the rocks and the dirt.

He was close by. He was *always* close by.

Panting, she scrambled over a boulder and slid down into the thorned canopy on the other side. Her delicate hands—unworked throughout her life—were torn and bloody, but it did not matter. Her knees ached, her ankle was sprained—pain she had never known before—and still it did not matter.

Because he was close . . . closer than he had *ever* been.

A chilling howl tore across the sky. She froze in the undergrowth, her heart hammering out of her chest and her breath heaving in protest as she tried to stifle it. She strained her ears.

The howl rang out again in glee and was accompanied by a scream that gurgled and faded.

Her matron was finally dead.

She felt it well up inside her, crimson light pulsating from her soul. The blood seeping from her wounds shimmered and rose from her hands as red vapour . . .

No.

She cut her urge short. *No.* He would find her if she did that. She hummed to herself, an ancient chant taught to her by the Sisters of Peace. The crimson vapour condensed into liquid and coagulated to cling to her skin, and the dark marks on her face receded to reveal the visage of a young woman once more.

The howl cried out again. He was coming.

In a panic she bolted through the undergrowth and tore into the open. The world was laid out beneath her; the bushland ended on a road that skirted a sheer cliff with a lush green glen spreading out below it. She skittered to a halt, sliding to the edge and waving her arms in a useless attempt to prolong her life. She was going over.

"Whoa there!" A yellow arm grabbed her by her torn robes, pulling her back from death to land on her arse. "Watch yourself there, miss. Could have been a nasty fall."

Laylen glanced up at her rescuer and recoiled. She was a warrior of some kind, tall and rippling with lean muscles, bound in leather armour with a bow at her back and an axe at her side. She had softly scaled yellow skin and long black hair tied half up in a knot with two tiny tusks protruding from her lower jaw. Laylen then glanced at her saviour's companions—a mismatched group of travellers, consisting of species the like of which she had never seen before.

"Are you with him?" Laylen cried desperately. "Are you with *him*?"

"Hey now there, little girl," the larger of the party said. He was tall like a tree and broad with pink, puffy skin, gnarled antlers, and a giant club over one shoulder. His voice was deep and powerful, but kind. "Are you in any kind of trouble?"

"Ah, she's just a stray. Let her run off." The next one to speak was more recognisable to Laylen.

He was short, standing only at chest height, and had a silver, pointed beard. He wore robes not unlike the sisters of her convent, but wielded brass gauntlets and had a litany of potions and vials strapped to his belt.

There was a human and an elf too, both male, and the only species of the party she recognised. The elf was adorned with a flowing white tabard and gold-trimmed pauldrons, while the human was decked out in plate armour with a mighty glaive.

"Get off it, Wuppet!" Another short creature emerged from behind the bearded one and slapped him across the head. She was much shorter than he was, with a bigger head and rust-coloured hair. She smiled broadly at Laylen, who shifted back in fright.

The yellow-skinned warrior turned back to her. "We won't hurt you. Was that howling from a beast? We can help."

Laylen pushed herself up from the ground and backed away from the outreached hand, shaking her head.

"Hey now, we're friends, little one," the big, lumbering one said.

"What, what are you?" Laylen finally croaked, timid, hoarse, and trembling.

"We're on contract to rid this area of a dragon . . ." the yellow one said. "My name is Prahtan, the ogre here is Ot," she gestured to the big one, "the grouchy dwarf is Wuppet, our helpful gnome is Gomlon, the human in plate is Myrrel, and the elf is Trestam. What is your name?"

"Ogre, dwarf, gnome," the girl said under her breath. "But *what* are you?"

Prahtan cocked her head. "You've never seen an orc before?"

"Orc?" Laylen sounded the word out and shook her head. "No, but I have read stories . . . Aren't you all supposed to be berserk?"

Prahtan giggled, deep but playful. "No, sweet human. Orcs don't go into a berserker rage unless they've feasted on a heart. Only, once you have your hand through the enemy's rib cage . . . going berserk seems kind of pointless." She smirked.

Laylen smirked back, the tension leaving her for a moment, but then the image of broken ribs and still beating hearts flashed through her mind and she recoiled.

"But you've never . . ." the dwarf called Wuppet hesitated, "you've never seen an ogre or dwarf or gnome before either?"

Laylen's eyes were still jammed closed to shut out the images of the last few days, but she shook her head.

Wuppet and Gomlon exchanged glances.

"Where are you from?" Prahtan asked. "What's your name?"

"Laylen," she finally said, "and you're all going to die." She turned and bolted down the path.

The six travellers watched her dart the bend around the bush in stunned silence.

"Anyone else feel ice shoot out their butthole at that one?" Wuppet asked.

"You're such a cock, Wuppet," Prahtan growled. "We should follow her."

"Cause she's a petite redhead human lass or . . ." Wuppet trailed off when Prahtan glared at him.

"What do you suppose she meant?" Ot's lumbering voice echoed throughout their very bones. "Poor thing looked petrified."

"Could it be the dragon?" Trestam asked.

"If it was the dragon, she would be smouldering and not bloodied. Something else is afoot." Prahtan unslung and strung her bow. "Let's be careful as we head down into the glen."

Wuppet cracked his knuckles through his gauntlets. "And here I was thinking a dragon hunt would be boring."

Prahtan looked down the path with worry. Her eyes darted through the brush that Laylen emerged from.

"What do you reckon, Prahtan?" Ot asked.

She sniffed and crouched down to the ground and shifted the dirt between her fingers.

"She's in her hunter mood, Ot," Wuppet sneered. "Won't get a word out of her."

"Can't you feel that?" Prahtan said harshly. "That tingling down your spine?"

"Not since I saw that hairy human woman in the last town . . ." Wuppet stopped jesting when Prahtan snarled at him. "Of course I feel it, Prahtan. The world hasn't been right since the War of the Damned. There aren't any necromancers to do their job anymore, and hauntings are running rampant. I can feel it in my soul . . . wrongness. But what does that have to do with our task?"

"To be fair, it's not like a previously benevolent dragon to swoop down on a town—a town without wealth, mind you—all of a sudden." Trestam scratched his pristine, rosy features. "This dragon was said to act out of altruism for the most part. Maybe everything is connected?"

"Now that is a bit much." Wuppet rested his fists on his hips. "Why would hauntings prompt a dragon to attack?"

"And if they did, would that not prompt more people to learn the art of necromancy?" Gomlon questioned, nudging Wuppet playfully.

"The first people brave enough to learn necromancy are going to make deadly mistakes without a master to guide them," Myrrel said. "And then the first ones to practice it openly are going to get lynched after what the old necromancers did. I do not think we can expect the hauntings to subside for quite a while."

"What do you think, Prahtan?" Trestam glanced at her, and his rosy face went taut. Prahtan was grimacing, her chest heaving as if she were in the throes of battle.

Prahtan fitted an arrow to her bow. "Ready yourselves. Something wicked this way comes."

Their demeanour shifted from playful banter to hard focus. Wuppet removed a vial from his belt and spread out from Prahtan. Ot growled and hefted his club, tapping the head against his mighty palm. Gomlon channelled crackling energy into her hands as Myrrel lowered his glaive. Trestam started chanting under his breath.

Prahtan's gaze darted, her years of hunting coalescing into the skill of bush sight. A twig cracked in the distance, and she saw the shape of the form that cracked it in her mind. A shifting brush, and she sensed its speed, its direction. A whiff of blood, stale mixed with new, and pheromones—as strange as they were—making her skin crawl. With that scent she knew the creature's intention.

"There!" She drew her bow and aimed to the left.

"Drawing a little early there, Prahtan?" Wuppet thumbed his vial open.

Her breathing rasped even as her muscles quivered under the strain of holding her bow drawn, but it did not matter. She had to be swift. This was something new.

Moments passed, and Prahtan's aim drifted with a quivering as it tracked the target, until finally, a being emerged. He seemed a man, tall, with a charming smile.

"Hello," he said, as normal enough as you might expect.

Ot growled and Myrrel shifted forward with his glaive.

"My, my, is that how you greet strangers in these lands?"

"Ones drenched in blood, yes," Wuppet returned.

"Ah." The man looked down at his robes, saturated with blood and chunks of flesh. "So sorry, still getting the hang of this disguise."

That's when Prahtan noticed it, the real thing that disturbed her about this . . . *man*. His chest didn't move as he spoke. He didn't blink or breathe or change expression; he just . . . *was*.

She let her arrow fly, and it tore through him, flitting into the brush behind.

"Now, now, I hadn't even threatened you yet," he tutted.

"Is it a ghoul?" Ot lumbered forward and readied his club.

"Can't be," Wuppet said as Prahtan hastily re-nocked an arrow. "There's no more necromancy."

"No more necromancy?" The man laughed, a chilling sound. "That's why we're here!" He . . . it . . . doubled over with a grunt, and his limbs convulsed. The sound of bone snapping and sinew tearing sent them cringing. The fresh droplets of blood that clung to its robes sizzled and evaporated into crimson vapour as the dried blood cooked itself.

"Wuppet," Prahtan ordered.

The dwarf flung a vial at the stranger, and it shattered at its feet. Red smoke surged upward to engulf it as the sickening sound of its body breaking and re-breaking itself continued.

"Get ready, Ot," Wuppet said as he brought up his fists into a guard, summoning spiritual fire around his gauntlets. "I don't think it brought him down."

Ot growled and surged forward, but hesitated as a new figure strode from the smoke cloud.

It was obsidian, tall and muscular, with red, monstrous eyes and a gaping, shifting red jaw of terror. Its face morphed with obscene horror, the crimson gaze inviting madness. Spines sprouted from its shoulders and down its back like a great trail of razor-sharp crags.

"Gomlon," Prahtan barked as she fidgeted with her arrow, her eyes wide, "when you're ready."

The gnome channelled the sparkling power in her hands and drew a rune in the air. It tore across the space between them and the creature and struck it with a flash of light.

"Ah," it growled, its voice inviting terror to the soul, warping the very air in a sinister, howling echo. Unperturbed from the attack, its shifting, insidious eyes homed in on the gnome. "A morsel to sustain me on my hunt." It reached out with its jagged claws, and crimson light shot from it. Gomlon paled and screeched in terror as she was dragged into the thing's grip in an instant. "Such a small amount of food." Its maddening jaw widened, and tendrils of magic were torn from the writhing, screaming gnome. Her body was desiccated as the life was siphoned from her and consumed by the creature, while shoots of red veins rippled across its obsidian body.

"Gomlon!" Myrrel screamed.

Trestam stepped forward and channelled the holy sunlight he had conjured into a lance that struck the creature's face. Wuppet leaped forward and struck it with a punch of spiritual fire. The thing flinched from both attacks, but then its hungry, maddening gaze fell back on them with glee.

"It's really cute that you lot tried to stop me. Even if the magic of the elf and the dwarf isn't something I can eat . . . yet." The party blanched as it spoke and discarded their dead companion, whose face was locked in terror. "Now which way did that little bitch run?"

There was a flash of blinding red light, and the creature screamed, flung away in a blast.

The five surviving heroes turned down the road, homing in on the source of the power. Laylen stood at the bend. Her arm was extended, and a dying red shimmer emanated from her.

"What magic was that?" Wuppet asked.

"Come on!" Laylen screamed. "More will be coming!"

"Lads, follow the girl," Prahtan ordered, and they bolted down the path towards Laylen.

"Thanks for coming back for us!" Ot cried as they dashed around the bend and down the cliff path.

Laylen was bounding as fast as her legs could carry her, but only managed to run a little faster than Wuppet, who powered along with his short, stocky legs. Myrrel and Trestam slowed to trail alongside him, and Prahtan brought up the rear with long strides, darting looks over her shoulder as the party surged on. Ot was at the front; each hulking step from the ogre rattled the ground.

"What the hell was that thing?" Prahtan shouted. "How could you stop it?"

"There's no time for that—more like him will be coming!"

"Why?"

Laylen turned with a pained expression, which morphed into horror, and she screamed. Prahtan looked back over her shoulder. The creature had stalked around the bend, howling and laughing from its red maw. But that was not what Laylen was screaming at.

Prahtan felt it before she heard it, a slight change in air pressure and then a beat from a giant, batlike wing.

"Down!" She tackled Laylen to the ground as Trestam, Myrrel, and Wuppet dived for cover.

Poor Ot turned at the call, and the flying creature collided with his face. It was obsidian like their initial attacker, with red eyes and a long beak that spat hellfire. Ot cried out in pain and tore it from his face, winding up his club and walloping it. His antlers were singed, but he was otherwise unharmed.

"What are these things?" Wuppet roared.

Sickly barbs shot out around them, attached to chains that rang out against each other as they were drawn back, raking at the earth and catching Wuppet and Laylen. Prahtan rolled aside and rose onto her knee. She drew another arrow and tracked the chains. The creature had extended an arm, and the black chains had shot from his hand. He was pulling the chains back now, along with his catch.

Prahtan drew and shot; the arrow smacked into its red eye with a thud. Its head snapped back, but it continued drawing the screaming Wuppet and Laylen.

"Shit, Ot!" Prahtan turned to find Ot was swiping at more winged creatures that swarmed down onto him. Myrrel was stabbing up in the air with his glaive as Trestam shot out lances of holy light.

The winged creatures were all different shapes. Some looked like wicked little men with claws and teeth, others like vultures, some like serpents. There were dozens of them, croaking in laughter at Ot's discomfort.

Prahtan gritted her teeth against her tusks. "Ot! Chains!" She drew and shot a flurry of arrows at the harassing creatures, each one finding its mark and, thankfully, doing damage. The arrows embedded in them, and they cried in shocked pain, swooping away or falling dead to the ground.

Ot took a moment to recover and grabbed the chains in a handful. His deep voice growled as he pulled, halting their inevitable reel back to their master. Wuppet was busy prying the barbs out of his robes, but Laylen was catatonic.

"He'll get me, he'll kill us all!" she kept repeating to herself. "I should have left you."

Prahtan slung her bow over her shoulder and pulled out her axe. "You should have, but you didn't. So I'm going to get you out of here." She reached for the barbs to find some had sunk into the girl's skin. "Shit, Wuppet?"

"I'm out!"

"Cover!"

Wuppet pulled another vial from his belt and threw it at the ground between them and the creature, then another on the path behind them, and a third into the brush. The thick red smoke engulfed the area around them. The flying critters did not swoop in, and the creature did not launch more chains.

"Hold him, Ot!" Prahtan hewed at the chain ensnaring Laylen with her axe. A red spark caused her to recoil, and the chain lengthened at the point of contact, coiling around itself. "No!" she screamed as she hacked again. "You will obey the laws of reason! You must!" She struck again, and again, and as the link weakened, it grew and coiled around Laylen's limb like a strangling snake. "Come on!"

Trestam channelled a lance of light in tandem with Prahtan's next strike. The link came free with a demonic howling. It recoiled as if in pain and retreated into the smoke. The lengthening end with the barb in Laylen was inert, for now.

"Finally!"

Prahtan looked around. There was nothing but the cliff face behind them, the creatures on either side and above . . . and the chain.

The things were swooping in again, harassing the party.

"Ot!" Prahtan threw the end of the barbed chain to the ogre. "We need your strength."

Ot growled in acknowledgment and wrapped it around his arm.

"Are you seriously suggesting we flee?" Myrrel roared, brandishing his glaive at the cloud.

Wuppet blanched. "Are you seriously suggesting we flee, *that way?*"

The dark shape of the creature emerged from the smoke.

"Quit your bitching and grab onto Ot, now!" Prahtan barked.

Wuppet, Trestam, and Myrrel obeyed, latching onto the ogre.

Prahtan steeled herself, ripped the barb from Laylen's skin, and jammed it into the ground, which cracked and groaned as the barb wormed its way in with dark power. Laylen was oblivious to the pain, shrieking and recoiling at the encroaching figure.

Prahtan wrapped her arms around the petrified human and held her close to her bosom. "You saved us; now let us save you."

Ot grabbed Prahtan and pulled her close too. "HOLD ON!" he bellowed and launched from the cliff.

The party left their guts and their groins upon the cliff, while the rest of them plummeted in a rushing torrent of air. Wuppet was screaming, and so was Laylen.

Prahtan bit down on her fear, and Ot growled, feeling the chain about to go taut.

With a crack they came to a jarring halt. They all grunted in shock, nearly losing their grip on Ot, who bellowed in agony. Prahtan looked around anxiously; they were only halfway down the cliff. She glanced up, ignoring the limp way Ot's extended shoulder stretched, the way the chain wrapped tightly around his arm, turning pink flesh purple, and she gazed up the cliff to find that the creature gazed back down at them.

It grabbed the chain in one arm and pulled, raising the party as if they weighed nothing.

"Forgive me, Ot!" Prahtan wriggled one arm free from his grip and struck at the chain links with her axe.

The chain writhed and grew as it did before. Each strike jolted the party with minor drops, and they cried out in small frights while Ot screamed constantly. All their weight was now hanging by the flesh between his arm and shoulder, the joint now dislocated for sure.

They collapsed onto a tent at the base of the cliff. Another party of people watched on from a distance, the commotion from above giving them time to retreat to a safe viewpoint.

Prahtan was up first. She grabbed Trestam from his tangle with Wuppet and roared, "Strike the chain with your light, now!"

Trestam grimaced and channelled holy light to his palm with a chant and grabbed the chain around Ot's arm. It sizzled and writhed and retreated from the arm just before being yanked up by the being above.

"What the hell is going on?" Wuppet upped and stormed from the tangle of bodies.

Prahtan handed Laylen off to Myrrel—who guided her away—as she and Trestam hefted Ot up to inspect his shoulder.

"What indeed?" The leader of the camp they had fallen into stepped forward.

He was an elderly orc with greening skin, a great white beard, and worn tusks. He had a hobbled gait and carried a gnarled staff. With him was a young, hooded satyr, a powerful-looking centaur clad in plate, and a goblin.

"Pardon the intrusion, Orc elder." Myrrel dropped Laylen and bowed. "We were beset by . . ." he choked, and his eyes darted around as the full weight of their encounter set in, "something . . . It killed Gomlon."

"Yeah," Wuppet shouted, "something!" He turned on Laylen, who huddled against a rock. "What the hell did you get us into?"

"Wuppet," Prahtan warned, "ease off."

"Is . . ." Laylen was rocking back and forth, "is he okay?" She glanced at Ot's arm and hurriedly looked away.

"His arm is dislocated," the old orc wizard hummed. "That was quite a feat, mighty Ogre."

Ot mumbled incoherently.

"Hush, Ot, hush." Prahtan caressed his face. "You did so well."

"Is he okay?" Laylen repeated.

Trestam was murmuring more chants and instilling healing light into the shoulder joint.

"Bah." Wuppet stalked from Laylen and pulled a salve from his belt, assisting with Ot's healing in his own stubborn way.

"Sometimes it's hard being so strong. People expect much from you and often give very little in return." Prahtan was still caressing Ot's face, smiling into his pain-veiled eyes.

"You speak as if from experience," Laylen said. "You have suffered?"

Prahtan gazed around the wrecked campsite. Myrrel was explaining with wild gestures the recent events to the people they disturbed, and Trestam and Wuppet were busy tending to Ot's shoulder. "These days, who hasn't?"

"Then why do you endure?"

"Because even these days, there is always enough hope." Prahtan went over to Laylen and hefted her onto her feet. "I think you owe us some answers."

"Starting with what the hell that thing was!" Wuppet barked.

Laylen jolted at his outburst. "He is an arch demon."

"An arch demon?" The orc wizard raised an eyebrow. He looked to his companions, who shrugged. "I don't think such things exist, my dear, not in this world."

"Sure as shit explains what we just witnessed!" Myrrel cried, his every gesticulation scraping his armour plating.

"He is a demon! He slaughtered my convent and has tracked me my whole life." Laylen sobbed.

"Why you?" Prahtan asked. "Is it to do with the magic you can wield?" Laylen looked away; Prahtan narrowed her eyes. "Why did we watch our friend get drained of life?"

"He and his ilk feed on magic. They crave it! They have been forcing their way into our world through the underworld in the weak spots of this plane. They seek sources of magic, and once they feed on them, the veil will weaken more, and more demons will pour through to feed on even more . . ." Laylen rambled.

"And why is this one hunting you?" Trestam asked.

Laylen looked away again.

"I may not have witnessed what you poor people have witnessed, but what the girl says makes some sense." The orc wizard hobbled over and inspected Laylen. "Without necromancers to keep hauntings in check, some places are more ajar to the underworld, where souls bereft of the great light may dwell. But demons . . . they are not something native to that place. The underworld is just an abyssal plane—the space between lights—an absence of peace and the sun. If demons exist, they are from somewhere else."

"They invaded the underworld centuries ago; they could easily breach the veil there. Now they seek to surge upwards . . . Wait . . . the necromancers are gone?" Laylen said.

The party halted and stared at her.

"You have been living under a rock, haven't you, honey?" Wuppet jeered.

"The last necromancers died a month ago at The Dwarf Islands," Prahtan explained. "It was a battle like no other, or so they say."

"And now with the failure of the necromancers to uphold their duty, the demons find our plane of existence unguarded?" Trestam wondered. "Will they possess us?"

Laylen laughed. "Possess you? No, the arch demon you faced is too powerful for your body to withstand. He has no need for your flesh. The lesser demons up there are too weak to dislodge your souls. No, they will not possess creatures such as us, only feed on your magic if you're lucky enough to possess it, or kill you horribly if you're unlucky enough to survive that long."

"Useless!" Myrrel barked. "This is all useless! We have to avenge Gomlon. I'll kill it . . . I can kill anything!"

"You are not yourself, friend." The centaur clopped forward and placed his hands on Myrrel's shoulders. "From one war master to another, control your breathing. Conquer your own animal to conquer the world."

"Get off me!" Myrrel knocked the arms from him and stalked back to the cliff, looking up. "I'll get up there and I'll kill that monster!"

"No power you possess can kill him," Laylen whimpered.

Myrrel turned from the cliff and chastised her. "What do you know? You've lived your life hidden away from the horrors of the world!"

"Easy," Prahtan said. "I sense there is more to this girl than we think."

"Oh, because she speaks to something in your heart?" Myrrel taunted. "Or stirs something a bit lower maybe?"

"Myrrel!" Trestam barked.

"Shut it. You all wanted to run when he was there waiting to be killed. I can kill him. I *will* kill him. All I need is a name. Tell me, girl, what is this *arch demon's* name?"

There was a rush of air. A dark figure dropped from the cliff and impacted behind Myrrel with enough force to shatter the stone. The creature—the arch demon—

landed on one knee and rose to tower over the quaking human war master.

Myrrel turned, his eyes so wide you could see them clearly through his visor.

"My name is . . ." the demon struck Myrrel's gut with his fist; it broke through plate, imbedded in intestine, and gripped around his spine, ". . . Carcenon!" He ripped and tore.

Myrrel screamed as his spine was ripped from his body; his head dangled from the vertebrae and lolled around as his limp body fell back, empty of nerve and substance.

"Shit!" Prahtan grabbed Laylen and threw her back from the cliff wall towards the thicket of trees.

The centaur cried out in shock but surged forward with spear and shield. His shaft splintered on Carcenon's obsidian flesh. With a deadly leer, Carcenon dropped poor Myrrel's spine and turned on the centaur, who reared up and struck out with his forelegs. Carcenon grabbed each leg with ease, halting the centaur's attack. With a sinister laugh, he ripped the forelegs and tore the centaur in half.

Gore and viscera jettisoned from the awful sight.

The orc wizard swirled magic with his staff and fired lightning on the demon, which crackled about his skin and caused the red veins to glow.

"Ah, more magic to feed upon!" Carcenon surged through the gore with thundering steps, took the staff from the orc, and shattered it. "I am still so hungry."

It happened again. The red light glowed, and blood sizzled into red vapour. The light flickered like crimson, ephemeral fire, hellfire. The orc screamed as his skin turned hollow and wisps of magic were siphoned from him into the demon's body. Then Carcenon discarded the body like it was garbage.

"Graw!" The goblin leaped over the desiccated carcass with his blade, which plunged into Carcenon's hideous red maw and sunk deep into his throat.

With a laugh, Carcenon bit down on the goblin's blade, tore the goblin's arm from his socket, and encircled his claws around the writhing amputee. "Embrace me, worm!" Carcenon squeezed and the goblin wheezed in pain as the life was crushed from him.

Prahtan and Wuppet ushered Ot after Laylen and begged the satyr to follow them as Trestam guarded the rear, conjuring light to his hands.

Carcenon squeezed harder, and with a crack and squelch, the goblin's innards shifted up and down, spurting from his lower half and oozing out of the orifices of his face.

With a satisfied sigh Carcenon looked to the satyr, who watched on with quivering legs. "You, I will take my time with." The demon stepped forward.

There was a flash and Trestam's holy light shot forth, striking Carcenon in the chest and knocking him back. "Move, satyr!" He grabbed the satyr's arm and sped away into the forest after his companions.

Carcenon found himself on his back with his chest sizzling, the crimson light within spilling out as the obsidian skin healed over rapidly. He gazed at the sky, where his minions circled down from the cliff above.

He stood as a little demon man with hobbled wings alighted by his feet. "They got away, sire. Master will not be pleased if he found out what you were planning here."

Carcenon growled and stomped the little demon to death. The others screeched and flocked away.

"My master need not find out about these plans until it is necessary. She is trapped here in the glen now. I shall hunt her and her new companions; make them suffer as I made her sisters suffer. And then, only once her soul is broken and her heart despairs, I will feed on her great magic! The hunt begins anew!"

PART IV

THE PREDATORS IN THE GLEN

The sky through the lush green canopy was clear, crystalline blue; the birds were singing and the crickets chirping, a wonderful day that may as well have been hell. The group trod through the brush and encroaching trees as if walking on eggshells. Every woodland creature that scurried across their path set them to react as if they had stumbled upon a hungry bear.

"Is he still tracking us?" Wuppet asked.

Prahtan hissed and knelt to feel the earth with her palm, her ears prickling to the sounds in the distance. Her bush sight came to her like a sixth sense, an amalgamation of her earthly perceptions into the impression of an image in her mind. Usually she used bush sight when tracking her quarry; now the hunter had become the hunted.

"Yes, he's just . . . strolling. He isn't even following our winding path or our decoy tracks. He's making a beeline towards us."

"He won't ever stop, not until he has what he wants," Laylen cried. "Your fate would have been less painful if I had just left you all to die on that ridge."

"You need more optimism," Ot's voice rumbled. "Why, whenever I am feeling down—maybe when some kids in a village ignorant of ogres give me grief for my appearance—I just stop and think on how lovely the world can be."

"That's all well and good when you didn't just watch your friends get torn apart!" The satyr who had joined them at the base of the cliff was sobbing.

"Hey," Trestam said softly, "we saw two of our friends die to that creature. Ot is just trying to help."

"I know, I know . . ." the satyr said. "I'm sorry, I'm just . . ."

"Shook." Wuppet spoke for him.

"Yes . . ."

"Well . . . the sky is lovely," Ot rumbled, "and I saw a deer over there. It had antlers bigger than mine."

"Yes, Ot, it was lovely." Prahtan bared her tusks pleasantly. "How is your shoulder?"

"It still hurts." He gingerly touched the pudgy skin where his shoulder had dislocated.

"Yeah, sorry, Ot," Trestam said. "We were interrupted before I could finish healing you. Luckily ogre musculature is strong enough to move around without the bone joint . . . for a time."

"Even with a skilled elven paladin to heal it, it hurts," Ot rumbled in reply. "I shall kill that thing if it tries to hurt any more of you."

"It won't work." Laylen started fretting again. "Nothing ever works."

"Hey, hey." Prahtan halted their march and took the young human mage by the shoulders. "You survived this far. We can do this."

Wuppet rounded on them. "Yeah, she has, 'cause she's got magic that can hurt the thing, maybe even kill him!"

"No!" she shrieked. "It always draws more of his minions."

"We can't keep stopping like this." Trestam sighed and rubbed his rosy brow. "Do we have a plan, Prahtan?"

"Yes." Prahtan gazed at him as she held Laylen. "There is a town somewhere over that way." She gestured ahead. "I wasn't going to take us through it with that thing on our tail, but I smell the pheromones of many warriors a way off, and more help would be . . . helpful."

Wuppet grated his brass gauntlets against each other. "Myrrel and Gomlon were warriors. It made little difference."

"We can't be defeatist, my grumpy dwarf friend." Trestam smiled. "Their souls now sail towards the great light of the sun to live in paradise."

"So why not just neck yourself if it's so grand up there, you pompous elf!" Wuppet roared.

"Hey!" Prahtan snarled as the elf paladin and dwarf monk squared up against each other. "We already have one unstoppable force bearing down on us! Let's not make it easier for it by killing each other." They backed down from their conflict with subdued grumbling. "Now I know we're rattled, but our best hope of surviving is to stay coordinated. We . . ." she trailed off and looked into the brush.

Ot rumbled a low growl and hefted his club, readying himself to defend from the direction she was facing.

"What is it now?" Wuppet pulled a vial of some concoction from his sash while Trestam channelled paladism into his hands and the satyr slinked into the shadows.

"Something else," Prahtan whispered as she nocked an arrow. "Carcenon is still tracking us from the way we came. But I smell similar pheromones in that direction, heading this way."

"More of those flying critters?" Trestam asked.

Ot whimpered and looked to the tree canopy, his face still scratched and singed from their swooping attacks.

"No." Prahtan closed her eyes and tried to form an image of the creatures bearing towards them with her bush sight. "They appear to be wolves. But they're larger, more sinister."

"Hellhounds," Laylen squeaked, tears running down her face. "Carcenon used them to flush us out from the convent, then sent them after the people who got away. If they're here it means they already fed on my sisters or worse."

"What are hell hounds?" the satyr asked from his hiding place. He was almost imperceptible in the brush. The party knew he was there for two reasons: they saw him go in, and he was speaking to them. The satyr must have been a rogue.

"Giant four-legged beasts with obsidian skin that has hellfire leaking through the cracks. It's like a crimson vapour-like fire, like . . ." she hesitated, "like Carcenon's power." She sniffled and stood up. "We have to leave, now."

"Damn it," Prahtan hissed. "We get to the village!"

"If those wolves are in the glen, it must mean our path ahead is compromised," Wuppet lamented. "The village could be in ruins for all we know."

"But the pheromones!" Prahtan protested.

"You know very well that a select few people can release that much battle pheromone if they're being slaughtered . . . They're done for," Wuppet countered.

"He's coming," Laylen whispered to herself, "he's coming, he's coming, he's coming. We can't stay here."

"All right," Prahtan conceded. "Satyr, what's your name?"

"Signat," his voice hissed from the brush.

"You head that way." She gestured towards the village. "We'll follow a few minutes behind you and cover your rear. If the village is still living, warn them of our arrival and our guests; if not, double back and we'll circle around the village on our way to the other side of the glen."

"You want me to go alone?" Signat's voice quivered.

Trestam smiled. "It'll be fine, friend. Our foes are not in that direction. Prahtan would sense them." A sigh hissed from the bushes, which rustled as the satyr snuck away. "Be careful," Trestam called after the rustling.

"All right," Prahtan said, "we form up, stay close. Laylen, do these hounds have any weaknesses?"

"Her magic, probably," Wuppet muttered.

"His minions aren't as impenetrable as he is," Laylen said. "They aren't arch demons, just hell folk and monsters. But hellhounds are as formidable as they are terrifying."

"So are we." Prahtan winked, and Laylen smiled back weakly. "We should be safe, don't you worry."

"I can still hear my sisters screaming as the hounds gnawed on them. Worry is too weak a word."

Prahtan hesitated, her yellow eyes lingering on the young mage, who glanced back nervously before her gaze flitted away. "I'll keep you safe," Prahtan finally said, "I swear it."

"Why?" Laylen's plea was a barely suppressed sob. "Why would you risk your life for me? You should just leave me here, let Carcenon take me, and run as far away as you can before his kind scour these lands."

Prahtan took Laylen's chin in her hands and directed her gaze back to meet her eyes. "Because I sense something in you worth fighting for." The words lingered in the silence, and she realised the other members of her party were watching intently. "Now, get up on Ot's shoulders. You can help us by being a lookout."

Laylen sniffed and shuffled over to Ot, who offered his good arm for her to climb up onto him. Once she was perched on his uninjured shoulder, she gripped onto one of his antlers as he ambled off. Wuppet grunted and followed Ot, while Trestam and Prahtan brought up the rear.

"You seemed to be taken with the satyr," Prahtan said.

"I like satyrs, grew up around them . . . You seem taken with that human," Trestam replied.

Prahtan bared her tusks in a guilty smile. "Well, like Wuppet mentioned, she ain't a hard thing to look at. And I do have a thing for her short red hair. But there's something about her, some scent I can't place. It's intriguing and frightening, especially given the situation."

"Well, maybe we'll find out soon enough," Trestam said.

"Maybe."

As they pushed through the mild undergrowth of the wooded glen, a chill crept over Prahtan. It had gone quiet. The birds stopped singing, and the woodland critters hid from sight. She paused and crouched again, letting her focus wander from her natural senses to perceive through her bush sight once more.

Carcenon—the arch demon that pursued them—she could not sense him, nor the hellhounds. But a foul scent scrunched her nose, and the trees hissed with an unnatural breeze.

With dread, she glanced up at Laylen, whose eyes darted around nervously.

"Ot," Prahtan roared. "Down!"

Ot instantly sprawled forward, and Laylen toppled from his shoulders to the dirt as a monstrous black creature leaped from the brush. Its jaws clamped the empty air where Ot's head was a split second before. Red, vaporous energy trailed in its wake, and its obsidian musculature was striated with pulsing red power.

It landed with the grace of supernatural agility, its paws gouging the earth with razor-sharp claws, and it snarled at the party with a drooling mouth. Each drop of viscous saliva hissed as it hit the earth. On all fours it stood as tall as Prahtan. She loosed an arrow, which glanced off its hardened hide with a defeated twang.

The hellhound rounded on her, taking its attention off Ot—who was still struggling to stand back up—and charged. Prahtan fell back onto her arse as the hellhound leaped through the air towards her. She loosed another arrow, which glanced off its snout, and moments before it clamped its mighty jaws around her body, it was blindsided by a lance of paladism from Trestam.

With a yelp it was launched away and slammed into a tree, rocking it to its roots and scattering the distraught birds hidden within its canopy.

Prahtan leaped up and drew her axe—closing in on the sizzling creature—and hacked at its eyes and jaw and charred skin, hoping to break through something. Her axe blade imbedded into the hellish skin—still smouldering from Trestam's attack—and it sunk deep. Glowing red viscera spilled out as the beast howled.

The howl was answered from the surrounding brush, and its pack mates closed in.

Prahtan swore and dodged back from the wounded hound's bite, then shifted back in to attack it again. She plunged her fist into the open wound she and Trestam had created and forced her arm deep into the creature's chest. The hellfire blood burned her skin, but her yellow orc scales could resist the heat for the moment. She forced fist through rib and organ as the hound wailed and she gripped its beating heart. She plunged her claws into it, and the creature whimpered as it died.

Ripping her dripping arm from the dead beast, she spun to check on her companions.

A hellhound leaped at Ot, but he had righted himself and walloped it with his mighty club. It collapsed with a snap and whimper, but a second hound leaped in its place. Ot lowered his head with a guttural roar and charged, skewering the new beast on his antlers as he surged forward and pinned its writhing form to a tree.

Trestam rolled over his shoulder and fired targeted beams of paladism into the rustling brush around them. They were smaller beams than the one he had used to save Prahtan, and he was already sweating and panting from the exertion. Prahtan loosed arrows where he fired, hoping they would penetrate the weakened obsidian after it was burned by holy sun fire.

Wuppet threw his vial bombs into the surrounding brush, throwing up smoke barriers of red and blue with a pungent odour that ruined Prahtan's sense of smell, but hopefully the hounds' as well. One lunged for him, and he chanted, summoning a spiritual barrier of orange fire that the hound's teeth cracked on. It reared up and cried in rage as Wuppet took the advantage, lunging forward to strike at the creature's underbelly with his brass gauntlets. The stubborn nature of the dwarf's limbs in tandem with brass gauntlets wreathed in spiritual fire—wielded with decades of martial training—sent the devastating punches ripping right through the hound's skin. Its hellish guts spilled out over the forest floor, sizzling through the soil with a sputtering hiss.

The desperate battle raged on like this. The pack of hellhounds attacked viciously and was continually repelled by the barest margins thanks to the party's skilled abilities and teamwork.

With several of their pack dead and dying around them, a hellhound howled a command, and the giant creatures receded into the brush. Prahtan's bush sight was addled by Wuppet's smokescreens and her raging nerves, and she could not sense how far they retreated.

"Is everyone all right?" she snarled, jamming her arrow into the eye of an incapacitated hound.

"My head hurts," Ot rumbled. The hellfire blood on his antlers dripped down and sizzled on his head before going inert.

"The hellfire only lasts a few seconds, Ot." Wuppet climbed up the ogre's arm and grabbed his antlers, wiping the burning blood with his gauntlets, which weathered the damage remarkably well. "There, should be all good."

"Thank you, grumpy Wuppet," Ot rumbled pleasantly.

"Trestam?" Prahtan took his shoulder as the elf doubled over and heaved.

"I'm all right," he panted. "Just knackered."

Prahtan's eyes darted around the battlefield. "Where is Laylen?"

"I told her to run," Ot said, "right before I broke this pup's spine." He lumbered over to the writhing hound he had walloped before skewering its companion. It whimpered and he roared as he caved its skull in with his club with two mighty swings. "She headed for the village."

"All right," Prahtan said, "we need to catch up to her. Whatever this Carcenon wants with her, we can probably bet he'll be more dangerous after he gets it."

The party stumbled out of the skirmish ground and through the brush after Laylen.

* * *

Laylen tore through the brush. The branches and thorns ripped at her face and garments as if they were the very servants of Carcenon, like they did on her flight from the convent. Only now she was also haunted by the sound of the rabid breath of a hellhound on her heels.

It barrelled through the brush and blindsided her, tackling her into a tree and knocking the wind from her. She collapsed in a heap and rounded as the hound recovered and bared its fangs.

She forced herself to suck in a breath of air and screeched, "Stay back!" She raised her outstretched hand, and the beast hesitated. Then it relaxed, its bared fangs hinting at a wicked smile. "I mean it!" She focused on the raging whim within her, on the need to let it out. Her eyes pulsed red, and she swam in a field of vaporous red energy for only a second. "You can't take me to your master if you're dead!"

The hound growled, its spine-like fur extended on end. It stalked forward, ready to attack, but was interrupted by the howl from the battle behind them. It glanced back at her and dashed into the brush with a dismissive snort.

Laylen breathed a sigh of relief as she lowered her shaky hand and allowed the dark power within to recede. She dragged herself onto her feet and bolted in the direction of the village that Prahtan had pointed out earlier. Laylen hesitated, considering going back to the party, remembering the deep colour of that orc's eyes, how her gaze held her like a gentle embrace . . . "No," she said. "The farther away from her I am, the safer she'll be." But she didn't know where else to go, so the village it was, and then out of this accursed glen.

After a frenzied half-an-hour-scurry through the woods, she came into a clearing to find a village constructed from the same dark lumber that made up the forest around her. It was silent, save for the sound of coursing water on the far side, up an incline that had wooden aqueducts snaking down towards the village. Smoke rose lazily from several chimneys within the walls, and the gates stood open. She sighed with relief and sprinted across the opening to the village gates and slipped inside.

As she entered the walls, her momentum halted, her blood turned cold, and a sickening feeling plummeted down her spine so suddenly, it rebounded up from her gut in the form of vomit.

The town was littered with the freshly defiled bodies of townsfolk. The buildings were wrecked, and the ground was gouged with the marks of struggle. Each gouge was filled with the still pools of blood that drained from the dead, who were skinned, dismembered, drawn, or strung up about the place in eerie stillness.

The stench hit her next, a stench more visceral than that of the hellhounds, as this was from creatures who once lived peaceful lives. They were men, women, and children of many races. Humans, elves, orcs, gnomes . . . and one satyr, strung up by his hooves within the town plaza. The satyr rogue she met at the base of the cliff, the one Prahtan sent ahead, Signat.

Laylen looked away from his pained, upside-down expression, dripping with his own blood and viscera.

She doubled over and tried to throw up again, but all that came from her pained effort was bile.

Carcenon most likely overtook them while he set the hounds on the others. He must have laid waste to this town in that short time and then had his way with the satyr like he said he would.

The post Signat was strung up from creaked, and the breeze pulled towards her, carrying the scent of his torment.

She wept, and in response to her misery, something within the town laughed at her. The voice was a sinister, howling echo that warped the very air.

"Do you feel guilty for their deaths?" Carcenon taunted. "They were luckier than my other victims lately, their deaths horrible, yes, but relatively quick . . . except for the satyr. What do you think I'll do to you when I finally feed on your soul?" He stepped out from the buildings and into the plaza. Tall, imposing, menacing, with obsidian-black skin cracked with the red power that drove him, and an insidious, shifting maw that pulsed crimson along with his madness-inducing eyes. He spread his arms. "Come, Laylen, let us end this farce, and maybe I will spare that orc wench you are so taken with by killing her quickly."

"I'll kill you!" Laylen screamed.

His laugh made her skin crawl. "We both know you don't have the power to challenge an arch demon!" He strode forward, each step rattling the buildings, rippling the puddles of blood, and shuddering her soul. "If you did, you would have saved your sisters, your matron . . ." She turned away and scrunched her eyes shut. "Oh, she did not die well." His insidious maw widened with glee. "And even if you did fight back, even if you could slow me down, more of my kind will be drawn to your magic. We will breach through the gaps in this pathetic realm, left unguarded by the hubris of your necromancers. We will consume the magic that sustains its barriers and then we shall march through in force and have our way with every disgusting overworlder we can get our hands on!"

He marched right up to her, and she backed away. She felt small, only as tall as his sternum. She also felt the brimming power within her threatening to rise past her inhibitions. She glared up at him. "I swear I'll kill you."

His laugh now filled her with dread, and he reached out with his clawed hand to stroke her face. "You are so adorable, little dem . . ."

Footsteps sounded behind Laylen. Carcenon hesitated and looked past her as Prahtan, Ot, Wuppet, and Trestam stormed through the gate.

They skidded to a halt, taking in Carcenon's towering form, the grotesque devastation of the village, and Trestam blanched at seeing Signat hanging by his hooves.

The elf channelled a bolt of paladism and launched it at Carcenon's maw. It struck the demon and he recoiled. Prahtan's arrow followed next and struck the base of one of his monstrous teeth; the shaft embedded in the gum, which was charred by holy light, and a tooth came free as he bellowed. Wuppet dived around Laylen, who stumbled out of the way, and caught Carcenon's falling tooth. He whipped it around and rammed it into the demon's knee and struck it with his gauntlets, hammering it in further.

Carcenon roared and collapsed. Ot lumbered in and struck a savage blow across his face with his club. With the sound of a titanic crack, the mighty demon fell back into the blood-soaked street with an earth-shuddering crash.

Prahtan grabbed Laylen, and the party sped past Carcenon's reeling form, sprinting across the grotesque plaza to the far side of the village.

"There's a bridge over a dammed river on the far side; if we can cross it and disable the bridge, we could halt his advance," Prahtan breathed between strides.

A dark shape swooped over them, and Carcenon landed with a grunt. He spun as Ot struck him again, and he caught the club with one hand. He slashed out with his other hand; demonic barbed chains lashed out from his arm and raked across Ot's belly. The ogre bellowed in agony and stumbled away. Wuppet leaped up next, and with a chant that conjured spiritual fire around his brass gauntlets, he punched into Carcenon's maw. The arch demon dodged the blow easily and caught Wuppet's wrist. With a deft motion he flung the dwarf over his shoulder, who then went skidding across the plaza.

Prahtan loosed an arrow into his maw again. He chomped it from the air and taunted her with a sickening grin, until a lance of light from Trestam knocked him across the plaza into the nearby tavern.

"Come on!" Prahtan hefted Laylen and rushed past Ot, who stumbled up, clutching his cut belly. She stopped when she realised Trestam wasn't following.

She turned to bark at him but hesitated, noticing how he looked up at the corpse of the poor satyr he was so enamoured by. "Trestam?"

"You get the others out of here." His chest heaved, and he summoned paladism to his fists. "I will hold him off."

Prahtan swore. She wanted to argue but knew they would be wasting precious time. She barked at Ot to heft Wuppet up, and they rushed out of the plaza and towards the gates on the other side of the town.

Trestam turned from the defiled body of Signat and faced the tavern he had blasted Carcenon into. "You'll pay for what you've done!" he roared, aiming his charging fists as beads of sweat formed on his brow like thick condensation. "You'll pay for what you've done to all of these people!"

Carcenon's insidious figure strode from the demolished tavern, and he laughed the same as before. "And who will make me pay, you? A mere elf who plays at true immortality? Or a paladin with all of the might of the sun coursing through his fingers but with a corporeal coil so weak, he pales to channel it? Come, worm, let us see who pays!"

Trestam was still channelling light, and the sun above dimmed as even the holy powers turned their attention towards his plea. His fists shook, the light lashed out in beams from the gaps in his fingers, and the sweat dripped from him and hit the earth like great drops of blood.

"In the name of the Holy Sun and its Guardians, I cast you from this realm, DEMON!"

He let his fists shoot open, and the lances of holy light pilfered the area like beams from the sun itself. Carcenon smiled and spread his hands before the twin lances smashed into him, knocking him back into the demolished tavern and beyond. The demon—charred and smouldering with pulsating hellfire—halted his tumble with a grunt and scrambled through the alleys around the tavern.

Trestam roared and with his power he strafed the whole area before him, the lances of light so powerful, so focused, that they cut whole buildings into halves. The structures collapsed in on themselves in clouds of dust and ricocheting chunks of wood, stone, and metal. The debris caught fire under the intense heat, and the whole town went up in a blaze. Trestam continued his vicious assault, firing light in every direction before him in his righteous fury.

The initial lances dulled and fizzled out, but before briefly thinking about collapsing, the beleaguered elf saw movement in the ruin. He spat blood and channelled smaller lances and bolts of paladism. He strafed the area again but now with sporadic power as the form of

Carcenon, damaged, enraged, but alive, sprinted against the barrage—towards Trestam—with thunderous steps.

Carcenon dashed to the side, and Trestam followed with his attack, fire and destruction raining in the demon's wake. His path skirted around the plaza as he spiralled in towards the elf, the holy light striking the rest of the town. Soon a thick, choking smoke filled the blue skies, blotting out the sun and throttling the air.

Trestam's rage fizzled out, and he collapsed onto his knees. Carcenon sprinted for him across the plaza, and in desperation Trestam summoned more light. He shot diminishing bolts of holy power at the demon, which struck him in the chest, face, and leg. But despite the damage it caused to his obsidian skin, despite the pained growl with every blow, Carcenon powered forward. As Carcenon closed in, Trestam channelled one final continuous beam with both hands. It struck Carcenon in the chest, but the demon surged through it to grasp the elf's hands and crush them in his grip.

Trestam moaned, too exhausted to scream, and the demon looked down at him with predatory intent.

"As you die," he growled, "know that not only did you fail your holy light, but it failed you." His jaw widened hideously, revealing rows upon rows of razor-sharp teeth all the way down his hellish throat, which ended in a black pit. "Once my master is done with this world, we will come for your precious sun. And if your soul makes it to your sun paradise, it means I will simply have the pleasure of devouring you a second time!" He paused, making sure that the elf had time to understand his words.

Then Carcenon's jaw grew wide and clamped down on Trestam. It was so wide, it engulfed Trestam's whole upper body. He crunched and tore with thousands of teeth and sucked the writhing elf down into his throat whole. Once he had finished feeding, his jaw realigned to his face. A wicked tongue lapped up the elf blood that still gushed from his mouth, and Carcenon looked up at the choking black smog, at the fire-red sun that shone through the hazy veil, and he howled in a victorious rage.

Prahtan, Ot, Laylen, and Wuppet turned at the sound of the vicious howling, looking down the rise to the village, which was now an inferno.

"He couldn't beat him," Wuppet moaned.

"He knew that," Prahtan growled. "He meant only to buy us time. Quickly, to the bridge. These aqueducts are from the dam. The bridge must be near."

Laylen paused as she moved past Prahtan. "I'm sorry!" she cried. "I'm so sorry!"

"Go!" Prahtan roared, and shot one last look back at the town. She raised her bow in salute to her fallen comrade. Not enough respect for her liking, but more than she had time to give Gomlon and Myrrel. Then she turned and sped after her party.

As they crested the rise, there were sounds of pursuit in the trees around them. Birds cried out and fled the trees, twigs snapped, and bushes rustled as beasts howled and brayed. The hellhounds closed in through the underbrush and were joined by the harpy cries of the winged critters that had attacked them earlier.

The party cleared the trees to find a ravine spanned by a sturdy wooden bridge. Further along the ravine the dam stood looming over them, built from rounded stones and mortar with a channel down the middle creating a pleasant waterfall. Wooden aqueducts ran from the dam towards the ruined town down the hill.

There was another howl. A hellhound lunged from the tree line, and Wuppet was quick to throw a vial that struck it in the face and exploded in a pungent yellow smoke. The hound whimpered and retreated as the winged critters swooped in. Ot was ready for them and swung out with his club, while Prahtan downed them with swift shots from her bow as the party crossed the bridge.

Laylen reached the other side first, and then Wuppet and Ot. Prahtan waited in the middle, shooting any of the creatures foolish enough to get too close.

"Destroy the bridge, Ot!" Prahtan barked.

Ot roared from the edge and swung at the bridge planks with his club, the whole structure rattling from his titanic strike. He roared and swung again, hammering away at the bridge, which shuddered and crumbled with every blow.

"What about Prahtan?" Laylen cried.

"She'll get here," Wuppet said, "just you watch."

Ot smashed the bridge again, and the whole thing shook violently. The hellhounds realised what was happening and leaped out from the tree line to surge over the bridge before it was destroyed. Prahtan turned and sprinted, and that's when they all heard it.

The clinking sound of demonic chains.

Several of them launched from the tree line on the town's side and caught Prahtan by the legs, arms, and waist. She cried out and collapsed as the chains encircled her and dragged her back across the trembling bridge, towards the rushing hounds, towards Carcenon.

Ot halted.

"Shit!" Wuppet clenched his fists and made to run across but hesitated when Prahtan barked.

"NO! JUST BREAK THE BRIDGE!" she snarled. "GET TO SAFETY!"

"What do we do?" Ot watched hopelessly as the hellhounds closed in on the ensnared Prahtan.

Wuppet's voice was a whisper. "We do what she says, break the bridge."

"No!" Ot blubbered.

"DO IT, OT!" Prahtan grabbed a plank of wood, but it ripped from its fixture as the chains dragged her to her inevitable death. "DO IT!"

Ot growled and then roared, hefting his club for the final blow. But he hesitated when chains shot out from behind them—from *their* side of the bridge—obsidian, hell-fired, demonic chains.

One of the chains swiped at the hellhounds, keeping them at bay, while the others encircled the chains restraining Prahtan and burned with vaporous crimson power. Prahtan's ensnaring chains writhed and released her, retreating back to Carcenon as the new chains grabbed Prahtan and hauled her to safety.

The orc hit the ground beyond the bridge, the chains unwrapped from her, and she looked up at her saviour, as did Ot and Wuppet as they followed the chains that receded and slunk back to their master, to Laylen. She was panting. Vaporous red power rose from her, red hellfire. Her eyes shone crimson, and she was baring her teeth in a grimace as the skin around her wounds dissolved, revealing dark, hellish skin in patches beneath her pale flesh.

Laylen strode past the party and gestured to the dam. Crimson lashes of energy shot from her and slammed into the stone structure, causing it to crumble and break. There was a sound like rolling thunder when the water burst from the cracks in the disintegrating structure, and then all at once the river that was locked on the other side broke free in a tidal wave. The rush of natural fury swept the bridge away in a flood with the remaining hellhounds. They howled in agonising panic before drowning in the coursing waters.

As the mists that rose from the churning waters cleared, Carcenon's dark figure became visible on the far side of the ravine, his skin healed already from his battle with Trestam.

He was smiling, and clapping. His hellish, warping voice rose over the torrents of the emptying dam. "Well, well, well, the bitch can bite worth a damn, it seems . . . and now every demon within leagues has sniffed you out. This valley will be swarming with hell folk by nightfall, and they will bring you to me in pain. I shall very much enjoy consuming you when I finally get my claws into you, Demon Princess!" He turned from the river and marched back into the tree line.

Panting, Laylen turned to face her companions. The vaporous energy subsided, her eyes dulled from crimson lights back to their natural blue, and her demonic skin was healed over by human hide. She looked away from them like a guilty pup.

"You're one of them," Wuppet said.

"You lied to us?" Ot rumbled.

"Laylen?" Prahtan picked herself up and cautiously made her way over to the human mage.

Laylen was weeping, and collapsed on the ground at Prahtan's touch. "I'm so sorry!"

PART V
DRAGON HELLFIRE

The party trod wearily through the flattening landscape as the smoke-clogged skies dimmed with the setting of the sun. It was quiet here on the far side of the glade; the birds did not sing, and the woodland creatures did not scurry. There was only the crunching of foliage underfoot, the rattled breath of the beleaguered adventurers, and the rumbling steps of Ot the ogre, who held his sliced belly with his good arm as his bad arm dragged his club in his wake.

"Explain," Wuppet had said back on the edge of the ravine, "now!"

Laylen looked up at Prahtan, who regarded her cautiously. The hunter didn't trust her—Laylen figured—but there was a hint of pity in those yellow orc eyes.

"You best do what he says," Prahtan said. "If we can't trust you, we can't let you run with us."

Laylen hugged her knees and rocked back and forth. "My mother," she sobbed, "my mother was one of the most powerful mages in history. She alone had the magical fortitude coursing through her body to survive being possessed by a greater demon . . . a demon like Carcenon or his superiors."

"There are greater demons out there than Carcenon?" Ot rumbled with concern.

"Oh yes," Laylen said, "far more terrifying as well. But one sought to breach this realm long before the veil weakened. Long before the necromancers shed their duty to guard those weak places between this world and the underworld. The demon king of Rarnc'l." She shivered. "He led the invasion from hell into the underworld. He rules over it now with a sadistic appetite and plays coy games with rival demon lords. He says his drive was always to claim the sun and the wealth of souls that rest within it. But my convent suspected he was being driven by something other than his own evil machinations. He saw a path between the planes through my mother. He sent his spirit to possess her, and over months she resisted his will with her might. She eventually exorcised him from her body, and he slinked back to the underworld to lick his wounds."

"So how did you happen then?" Wuppet said.

"My mother was already pregnant with me when Rarnc'l tried to dislodge her soul. With the hellish powers coursing through her—counteracted by her own magic defences—something must have happened in the womb. In the place where her body fed mine, I was exposed to demon-hood as if I was being grown within one. I am told I would have died or been born a thing of pure evil had I not been my mother's daughter." Laylen sighed and looked away.

"So you were born with this curse?" Prahtan prompted.

"Yes, and whenever I lost control, whenever I used my dark power . . . well, it would be like a beacon to all the demons that had already slipped into this realm. My mother died defeating two arch demons single-handedly, weakened by waves and waves of their minions. The convent took me in after that and taught me how to conceal my might. So that's what I did. If I were to use my power, they would be drawn to me, to kill me and feed on my magic, and the ones around me would suffer worse fates. So that's what I did. I made myself meek; I became this small, pathetic thing to keep myself safe."

Ot grumbled and leaned on his club. Wuppet rolled his eyes and turned away, crossing his arms.

"What are you going to do with me?" Laylen asked in their silence.

Prahtan regarded her for a long moment. "You know," she said softly, "that isn't what meek means."

"What?"

"Meek, it isn't being weak, or pathetic. To be meek is to possess terrifying strength, but to have enough control over yourself to never have to use it. And when it is used, it is wielded righteously." She paused and laughed. "So I guess you really are meek. Meekness is strength under control. In my culture, it is a great honour to be branded as meek." She reached out and helped Laylen to stand; she took her by the shoulders and gazed into her soul. "You have suffered untold atrocities, and yet you have reined yourself in to protect those around you. You are pursued against your will by foul creatures, but when it came to it, you unleashed your power to save me and my friends. Your power might be like a beacon to the demons of the world—to things that would swoop in to tear it from you—your power might make you feel vulnerable, but you possess much might. You are strong enough to be vulnerable, dear, sweet Laylen." She embraced Laylen warmly. "You can shine your light and fight off the wicked things that seek to snuff it out at the same time."

"I'm . . ." Laylen's breath seized and she suppressed a sob . . . *Strong enough to be vulnerable.* The words echoed in her mind.

"Hush now, little human." Prahtan squeezed her tightly and released her. "We have a demon on our tail, and if he was telling the truth, we have many more on the way. We must soldier on."

That conversation was hours ago now, by the coursing ravine and the broken dam. Now they trudged into a deep gouge in the earth, scorched raw and marked by the withered black husks of trees.

"What is this?" Laylen asked, a charred branch snapping beneath her feet.

"Dragon," Wuppet snarled. "We were so preoccupied by the demon tracking us that we forgot we were hired to rid this glen of a bloody dragon!"

Prahtan knelt in the ash and sniffed the scorched ground. "This boundary was burned out two weeks ago." She gazed down the trench and cocked her head. "It was drawn by a single line of fire, forming a large perimeter in this section of the forest."

"Dragons are territorial," Ot rumbled. "Makes sense."

"But it doesn't," Prahtan said. "Dragons are territorial, yes, but one large enough to carve this much out of the forest with its fire would occupy the whole glen, not this little piece of it . . . Something is amiss."

Wuppet cracked his knuckles. "Well, this dragon is a strange one. It was said to be a recluse on White Sun Peak some fifty leagues from here. Never attacked anyone, never hoarded anything. Then all of a sudden, it swooped into this glen and drove out two villages . . . which I assume reside somewhere within this perimeter."

"It's protecting something then," Ot said.

"But what?" Wuppet turned on him. "What reason would a dragon have to . . . Ah, shit."

"What?" Prahtan said.

"Those demons are out to consume sources of magic, right?" he asked Laylen.

"Yes?" Laylen answered.

"You said that once those sources are consumed, the realm will unravel more, which means more demons will be able to cross over into this world?"

"Yes?"

"The dragon must have moved in to protect a source of magic then." Wuppet sighed. "Trestam was right, it was acting out of altruism after all . . ."

Prahtan snarled, "Carcenon is still on our trail. We have no choice but to continue forward. Maybe this dragon could prove an ally?"

"I doubt it," Ot rumbled. "What we need to decide is whether it's better to die by dragon fire, or hellfire."

"What is dragon fire like?" Laylen asked.

"It sears you so intensely and so swiftly that you're aware of flesh and muscle melting off your bone and your marrow baking within it . . . or so the stories say." Wuppet laughed.

"Dragon fire is the better death then." Laylen nodded grimly. "Let's get this over with."

The party silently set off as the red sun fell past the edge of the world and twilight turned to morbid night. It was cold now. The stars were veiled by the haze from the burning village, and the moon shone a sickly yellow glow through it all.

They reached another clearing, in the middle of which was a large grass mound. The peak of the mound was punctuated by bubbling brooks that spilled from the top in different directions; their paths were pockmarked by ancient druid stones. The stones were marked with ancient runes, carved deep and thick into their cores. There was a mountainous rock on the far side of the mound, imposing compared to the druid stones. It was smooth and out of place.

"Water," Ot rumbled.

"That looks like a defensible position to camp." Prahtan gestured to the top of the mound fortified by the druid stones.

"A defensible position, yes," a gargantuan voice echoed out throughout the hallowed space, keening from the stones and rattling the cavities in their chests, "but not a camp for the likes of you."

The dark, mountainous stone on the far side of the mound shifted and expanded. It spread great membranous wings that could canopy the whole clearing, and a great serpentine head slinked out from beneath them. Uncoiling, the dragon of the glen spread to its full span and rose over the mound like a giant breaking wave.

"Well," Wuppet sighed, "shit."

"We can take it," Ot rumbled. "It's why we came here in the first place."

"When we were three more strong, and with all of our stamina, and without an army of hell chasing us," Wuppet lamented. "Face it, friends, we're doomed."

"Doom?" The great dragon's voice boomed from the stones again, and its head stooped low over the natural fountain. It had white claws that reflected the sickly moonlight, with black membranes across its wings that added to the depths of the thick haze. They could just make out its deep amber scales in the gloom, and the dimness was punctuated by the glint of its fiery yellow eyes. "You have brought doom to many, dwarf. You have led the enemies of this world straight to the magical font I came to protect. Now this whole continent may be lost if I cannot repel the demons. If I fail to prevent them from consuming the font, this glen will become a staging ground for the first great invasion of hell into the world."

Laylen pushed forward from the party and quivered as the dragon regarded her with predatory features. "Great dragon!" she cried. "Your kind is said to possess incredible might. Can you not win against Carcenon with the aid of my friends here?"

"So Carcenon is his name? We will fight the great duel of our age then. If the swarms of his minions don't overwhelm you as we do battle, then they will at least keep you occupied enough to prevent you from aiding me."

Carcenon's sinister laugh echoed throughout the forest behind them. The dragon growled and bared its spear-like teeth as the party recoiled up the mound.

"Speak of the wicked!" Carcenon's voice warped the very air like a plague on reality, and his insidious form trudged through the woods to halt at the tree line. "And I shall appear!" He was a tall, imposing figure in the darkness, with obsidian-black skin laced with veins of crimson hellfire, and broad shoulders with wicked spines that ran down his back. His nightmare face leered at them, crimson jaw gaping and drooling with anticipation and his shifting, maddening eyes regarding them all at once. "How lucky for me. I set out to track down Rarnc'l's little bitch, to take her power for my own so I can claim my rightful place in the upper echelons of Hell's court, and what do I find? A central font of magic! Once I consume that, I will be exponentially more powerful . . . *and* a dragon? Perhaps Rarnc'l might even forgive me for claiming his daughter's power if I bring him the possessed body of such a mighty creature!"

"You will not claim my body, nor this magic, you foul mould of consciousness!" The dragon reared and spread its wings; the gust that they wrought bent the trees and knocked the party to the ground, but Carcenon remained still. "I will smite thee like the hammer smites glass. You will shatter in my grip; you will break under my jaw; you will writhe within my fire!" The dragon inhaled, and a foreboding orange glow pulsated from its throat. "I AM AMBARON, THE BLAZE OF RIGHTEOUS FURY, AND I SHALL BURN YOU ALL!" It breathed a jet of intense orange fire from its maw.

It struck Carcenon and blew out past him, igniting the trees in a cone of fire and illuminating the hundreds of lesser demons that were hiding in the desiccated woods. They screeched and scurried away from the blast, but Carcenon—inflamed and screaming in rage—leaped through the air from the inferno to strike at the dragon.

"Do not let his minions reach the font!" Ambaron ordered as it struck the streaking form of Carcenon with its tail midair. The two beings became embroiled in a fierce exchange of dragon and hellfire as their brawl spilled from the top of the mound.

The other demons swarmed from the tree line and up towards the undefended font. They were of every possible visage imaginable: great hellhounds, serpents, deformed little men, hawks, and many more indescribable beasts.

Ot roared and charged into the mass, swinging his club in a wide arc and splattering many of the lesser demons. The larger demons dove around his swing or swooped down from on high.

Wuppet chanted, channelling spiritual fire into his brass gauntlets, and he went to work in Ot's wake. He struck at the demons that evaded the ogre's blows and threw his powder-infused vials into the fray to disperse and disorient the hell folk.

Prahtan pushed Laylen back and shot at the flyers with her diminishing arrows. She aimed for the pulsating red marks on their obsidian skin, or for the eyes, or the jaws—which all seemed to be weak points.

Laylen shrieked as a hellish bull charged up towards them both. Prahtan snarled, drew her axe, and leaped through the air to meet the bull head-on. She struck with the might of all the orcs and cleaved its skull in two.

"Laylen!" She turned and snarled, "Can you fight?"

"I'll only draw more of them!" Laylen cried back.

"Then get out of here!" Prahtan ordered, kicking back an insidious creature that resembled a giant squid with a serpent's tail. "Get out of here and don't let the bastard consume you!"

Laylen looked helplessly across the clearing as more demons swarmed in and up the druid stone mound. Ot was becoming overwhelmed, unable to fight so fiercely with all of his injuries. Wuppet and Prahtan closed in to support him, but even with their great prowess and abilities, there were just too many demons.

Across the clearing, Ambaron and Carcenon raged against one another in a titanic clash. Carcenon would lash out with his chains and his claws and his hellfire. Despite his small size compared to Ambaron, he was still fighting with enough force to make the dragon recoil in pain from his blows.

Ambaron would return with its own bouts, bashing with wings or tail, biting at Carcenon's form or gouging at him with its claws before unleashing a torrent of amber fire from its maw. As the battle raged on, its scales were cracked, its body was bled, and Carcenon—despite weathering much damage himself—persisted.

With every blast of fire, the dark skies were illuminated, revealing hundreds more winged demons that circled overhead. They swooped at opportune moments to attack Ambaron or Ot. Or they would try their luck and dive for the magical font before Prahtan shot them down or Wuppet dissuaded them with a well-placed vial throw.

With a swing of his hand, Carcenon cast forth his hellish chains, and they pierced through Ambaron's body and out the other side in three points like deadly lances. Ambaron screamed in pain and collapsed—shaking the earth upon impact—as Carcenon yanked him into the dirt.

Carcenon's deadly laughter boomed. "Now, Dragon, now your body shall be mine!"

The arch demon dissolved into vaporous hellfire and seeped into Ambaron's wounds. The dragon writhed and resisted but had been weakened. The beautiful amber scales charred to obsidian black, hellfire leaked from its wounds, and its eyes burned from yellow to crimson.

Carcenon rose in Ambaron's form and roared. The demons attacking the party shrieked and recoiled, receding back into the tree line to clear the way as the demonically possessed dragon lunged for the party of defenders. With a slash of its mighty claws, it raked Ot aside, almost cleaving him in two across the chest. Ot went flying back against a druid stone on top of the mound, with Prahtan pinned behind him.

Laylen blanched and shrieked, rushing for her downed companions.

Wuppet snarled and threw his final vial. It struck Carcenon's snout, and a yellow gel clung to its nose and eyes. It roared and breathed a heretical combination of hell- and dragon fire at the dwarf, but Wuppet chanted and produced a shield of spiritual fire around him like an orb. The blast flowed around him, leaving him untouched. With a roar Wuppet lunged at the blinded dragon and struck out with all the spiritual fire he could muster into his blows.

As Wuppet distracted Carcenon, Laylen reached Ot. Prahtan was pulling herself from behind him, mostly intact. But Ot . . . his chest was a gaping wound, his ribs were cracked, and his beating heart pulsed visibly beneath the gore.

"Oh spirits," Laylen cried and retched. "Oh spirits, oh no, Ot." She collapsed at his feet.

Prahtan snarled at her. She was in pain too but grit her teeth through it. "Why are you still here? You need to run!"

"I can't just leave you!" Laylen screamed.

"You can't stay here either! We're going to lose." Prahtan glanced at the fight between Wuppet and Carcenon.

Carcenon had Wuppet in its jaws, clamping down on the dwarf, who held out with a shield of spiritual fire.

"You can win," Ot moaned weakly.

"How, Ot?" Prahtan hissed. "No power can defeat that thing." She looked up in despair at the demons that swarmed and watched the struggle like a deranged match.

"Take my heart," Ot mumbled. Laylen and Prahtan stopped and looked at him. He gestured to his chest. "Take my heart, embrace the berserk rage of your people . . ."

"Even if she did that," Laylen wept, "there is no guarantee she will win."

Ot smiled weakly. "There is never a guarantee, little human. The world is dark and full of horror, and sometimes it seems like nothing can defeat it. But the good must still try, and in trying they discover that they are strong enough to face the world's woes. The fact that I have lived a life of love is a testament to that . . . Prahtan saved me when I was just a teenager, against fearful odds. We are proof that fighting for life can reap its own rewards."

"Ot," Prahtan stroked his face, "I can't just . . ."

"Do it!"

Behind them, Carcenon threw its head back and swallowed Wuppet whole.

Prahtan snarled—and reached into Ot's chest. She gripped his heart and wrenched it free with a wet snap. Ot cried out in shuddering agony and then went still. Panting, Prahtan brought his still beating heart to her lips and bit into it with her tusks.

The change was sudden and terrifying. Prahtan's limbs trembled, and her muscles pulsed and swelled, vascular and bulging even under her light scales. Her eyes rolled back into her head, their lovely yellow replaced by an orange-veined sinisterness, and she turned on the dragon that now regarded them.

Prahtan cried out a mighty, guttural roar that caused Laylen to jump back in fright, and charged the enormous dragon with nothing but her axe in hand. She leaped through the air and struck its head with such force that it reeled, crashing into the ground with a titanic quake.

Laylen watched in shock, not even glancing back at Ot's still body as Prahtan laid waste to the dragon in her vicious, berserk rage.

But despite her immense berserker strength, she would fail. Carcenon would consume her with glee, and the demons would devour the magical font so their kind could invade the world.

Laylen could not let that happen. She could not let Prahtan die. It was time she stopped hiding.

As Prahtan's attacks weakened—as Carcenon gained the upper hand and used his terrible new body to overpower the raging orc—Laylen climbed up atop a druid stone. She repeated the mantra Prahtan had instilled in her. That she was strong enough to shine and fight off the evils that would seek to snuff her out. She repeated the words that had brought her to tears.

"I'm strong enough to be vulnerable." She gripped the patterned stone with trembling hands and climbed. "I'm strong enough to be vulnerable." Carcenon clamped its jaws around Prahtan and shook her like a rag doll before throwing her down at Ot's body. The orc cried out, bleeding from several gouges in her tough yellow hide, but she still snarled as the dragon bore down on her. "I'm strong enough to be vulnerable." Laylen stood atop the stone, watching the flank of the dragon as it bared its fangs to end Prahtan. She gazed out over the flocking demons and the insidious critters that lurked in the tree line. She shuddered—knowing what she was about to do—and repeated once more a battle cry of her own, "I'M STRONG ENOUGH TO BE VULNERABLE!" She widened her stance, raised her arms, and roared. For the first time in her life, she unleashed the full might of her power.

A lance of bright crimson beamed from her core and tore into the smoke-veiled sky. The power was so forceful, it parted the smog and allowed the stars and moon to shine into the glen in full radiance. Her eyes pulsated with red, her form swam in the bloodied, vaporous power of hellfire, and the obsidian skin beneath her human veil crept out in patches around her wounds.

Carcenon halted before his teeth clamped onto Prahtan, who recoiled and gripped Ot's body with her eyes jammed shut against her coming doom. She pried them open as Carcenon snarled a smile and turned towards the crimson beacon of power.

The other demons cried out in glee and swarmed towards the demon princess from the tree line and from the sky, and Carcenon followed suit.

Laylen smiled sinisterly and roared again. She leaped into the sky with a thunderous sound and struck the demons in their scores with jets of crimson hellfire from her hands. She raked at the ground with her insidious chains and blasted the charging dragon with all of the might of hell untempered.

Carcenon was knocked to the ground while the demons died in droves, even as hundreds more swarmed the beacon that was Laylen, drawn to her terrible power.

Prahtan watched in awe as Laylen fought off the hosts of hell with brilliant displays of dark magic. Carcenon rose again and she streaked down into him— colliding with the scaled creature like a meteor—and a crackling flash boomed throughout the entire glen.

When Prahtan could blink her vision back into focus, she found Carcenon wrecked upon the mound and the other demons fleeing in terror even as Laylen struck them from the sky.

"I am Laylen, daughter of Casessa!" Her voice filled the night, and she turned on the writhing dragon. "By my might I cast you out, Carcenon!"

She made a pulling gesture, and the vaporous hellfire was drawn from Ambaron's form. Its amber scales returned to their previous lustre as the demon was exorcised, and it breathed a sigh before collapsing, unconscious. Carcenon's kneeling form pooled before Laylen when she landed and stood over him.

"You can't win!" He writhed in her demonic grip, kept on his knees, keening in pain. "More of my kind will come through!"

She waved her hand and his body dissolved from his feet up—slowly—and he screamed the whole time while she laughed.

"You will be dismembered, and your spirit will slink back to the abyss you crawled out of, weak, humiliated, and fearful. Report back to your master that YOU FAILED!" She clenched her fist, and his writhing intensified. "I will seek out all of your kind foolish enough to rear their heads within this realm and kill them at my leisure!" She pulled her fist down, and Carcenon pulsed with red light, his body shattered, but the image of his torso and pained face remained in vaporous form, watching Laylen in horror. "And when your pathetic kin realise the danger and flee from this realm in fear, I will use my dark gifts to instil necromancy into a host of my own. I will have them stand guard at all of the weak spots in this realm and chant of your kind's failings, to be heard everywhere from the depths of hell to the highest peaks of the sun as I follow you into the underworld and dismantle you all! I will find your demon *king*. I will eviscerate him and use his entrails to seal the portal between hell and the underworld. Your kind will fail and recede into oblivion once more! I'll . . ."

"Laylen!" Prahtan's desperate voice cried out from below. Laylen's eyes flickered from red to blue, regarding the orc huntress. "Laylen, that's enough, it's okay . . . You've defeated them."

"I . . ." Laylen glanced at Carcenon's writhing image and waved her hand. His form dissipated into the depths of the underworld, and she gouged at her face, collapsing onto her knees and wailing, "By the spirits, I'm a monster!"

Prahtan limped over to her as dawn crept over the edge of the world, soaking the darkness in light. She embraced Laylen. "No, no, not at all." She held her close, wrapping her limbs around the sobbing human. "You saved us, dear Laylen."

"But I let Ot die. I let all of your friends die! And I relished in the pain I caused those fiends. I'm just as bad as they are!"

"Hush, hush," Prahtan cooed. "Ot lives."

"You ate his heart!"

"Ogres have three hearts." Behind them, Ot stirred from unconsciousness. "His adventuring days are over, but he can still lead a long, happy life," Prahtan smiled, "because *you* saved us. You were brave enough to reveal your might to the world, you were strong enough to be vulnerable, and you were victorious."

Laylen looked up into her eyes. "I . . . I . . ."

Ambaron stirred and hissed. In the dawning light its scales shimmered brilliantly even as they were cracked and marred. It coughed—retched would be a better word—and a little creature wreathed in an orb of spiritual fire tumbled out from its mouth in a heap.

"Wuppet?" Prahtan cried. "You survived!"

Wuppet coughed and spluttered. Ot slowly lumbered over to check on him, gripping his gaping wound as he went.

"You freed me," Ambaron's gargantuan voice reverberated throughout the clearing, "and in doing so have revealed a new danger. I should kill you, demon spawn."

Laylen stepped before Prahtan to face the dragon. "You should, but could you?" She pulsed with hellfire menacingly, and the dragon snorted dismissively.

"A fair point to make." Ambaron slinked low and rested its head. "Perhaps I should heal first, and if by then you have proven to be a threat, I will hunt you down."

"I will be waiting," Laylen said. "Wuppet, Ot, are you all right?"

"I feel like this is the worst hangover I've ever had," Wuppet groaned.

"I am in pain, but I still live," Ot rumbled.

Laylen nodded and turned back to Prahtan. "What of you? Your wounds look fierce."

"My wounds were sustained during my berserk state; they should scar up nicely." Prahtan bared her tusks pleasantly and took Laylen's hand, caressing it gently. "You were incredible."

Laylen looked from Prahtan's tusks and up into her wonderful yellow eyes. "I wouldn't have been without you to believe in me." Her eyes half closed, her lips parted.

Prahtan inhaled deeply and leaned in, brushing her lips against Laylen's.

"Ow." Laylen inched back, giggling. "Your tusks . . ."

"Oh, sorry." Prahtan laughed. "I've never kissed a human before."

Laylen giggled. "We'll figure it out together."

They nuzzled against each other as the dawn turned to brilliant morning, over a glen cleansed of evil.

PART VI

EPILOGUE: HELL WRATH

The black halls echoed with the sounds of screeching laughter. Carcenon "The Broken" was dragged through the court of Hell upon jagged chains, his once imposing figure withered into that of a pathetic imp's.

The Lord of Hell sat upon a throne of red stone, a lean, lithe figure of obsidian black with an imposing crown of sharp barbs. He stood twice as tall as an arch demon, his limbs long and bony and pulsing with hellfire.

"Carcenon, my faithful servant," the voice rumbled from the walls.

Carcenon doubled over in pain at his master's voice, writhing in agony as the gathered masses of demons and lesser demons jeered at his suffering. Lining the upper levels of the court were balconies, red lit and garishly contrasting the pitch dark walls. Arch demons watched silently from these vantage points, their maddening eyes shifting between their lord and their former rival.

"My King Rarnc'l!" Carcenon pleaded. "I did not know the demon princess guarded the font!"

The voice rumbled off the walls again, a deep, rolling laughter that wedged madness into Carcenon's mind, his nightmare jaw twisted and broken with dark magic.

"Oh, Carcenon, my little pet, I have already broken your minions within my pits. They told me *all* before I damned them to the eternal fires. You sought my daughter out for her power. You only happened upon the font by chance. I sent you on this mission to find and break the fonts so that our legions could pour into the overworld.

"Your reward would have been to ingest the magic that dwelled there. Was this not enough for your ambitions? Did you really seek to contend with my strength by absorbing my daughter's power too? You fool!"

Rarnc'l rose from his throne and strode down into the court itself. The lesser demons shrunk back as if his closing presence was a lash of flame.

"YOU FOOL!"

He struck Carcenon across the face, and his jaw dislodged with the blow. It went clattering into the masses of lesser demons, who devoured it within seconds. "Why did you think that my daughter's power would lend you such an advantage, yet at the same time you hunted her like she was a lesser? I do not begrudge you your selfish ambitions, my putrid little servant, but I do begrudge that you let your ego cloud your judgment. Now my daughter knows her power; now she can guard the fonts against as many demons as we can send through the breaking veils . . . Soon more necromancers will arise to safeguard those weakened places, and the Dark *still* presses in!"

"A true king would not flee . . ." Carcenon spat from his bleeding maw, able to speak due to the infernal nature of Hell. He gazed upon his tormentor in defiance. "Perhaps your daughter should lead us against the Dark. She sure wept less than you in the face of utter destruction."

The court went silent—all laughing, all jeering ceased as Rarnc'l looked down upon his broken servant. His body seemed to grow taller without moving, the king's shadow darkening over Carcenon's body.

"The Dark wants what is beyond our veil . . ." He reached down and grabbed Carcenon by the neck. "I was not always king, my faithful servant, but I was

there when the first ruler of Hell fell before its might .
. . We only live now because I could reason with it. All
we have to do is create a path for its ascension, and we
can live in its wake. It does not rest, it does not stop,
and if it achieves its goal without our aid, then it will
consume us like it will all the rest . . . *if* we are lucky.
You, Carcenon, will not be so lucky."

Rarnc'l turned with Carcenon still in his grip and
strode back to his throne, passing around it, and went
through a darkened chamber. The lesser demons did
not jeer as Carcenon struggled against his master. Even
they would not wish such a fate on their worst enemy.

"No!" Carcenon pleaded. "Send me to the eternal
fires, send me to drown in the acid reefs, anything but
this, please!"

"If you want someone to lead us against the Dark,
my servant, why not take on that role yourself?"

Rarnc'l pushed past a door of twisted iron. Beyond
it there was a circular chamber with an abyssal well in
the centre. Darkness ebbed and flowed from the edges
of the well as if it was water. Despite the fires of Hell,
despite the screams of the tormented, this room was
cold and silent.

"Please, Rarnc'l, don't do this. I can atone for my
sins against you! Send me back through and I will
break the fonts. I will tear open a breach in the veil so

large that even the greatest demons of Hell can surge through, please!"

Rarnc'l lifted Carcenon so that he could press his lips into the demon's ear. "Carcenon, my pet, I would have subjected you to an eternity of torment for your failures . . . I was willing to be merciful for you . . . but you *had* to challenge my rule in front of all the others. And so now I consign you to the Whims of the Dark. Whatever horrid fate it twists you to, I hope that you have enough of you left to one day forgive me."

"My king, no!" Carcenon pleaded, but Rarnc'l threw him into the dark well.

Carcenon splashed into the impossible waters. Thousands upon thousands of dark hands reached out from the abyss and ripped strips of flesh from the former arch demon, who screamed in agony. His blubbering voice was throttled as he was dragged beneath the dark depths.

Silence filled the well room once more, and Rarnc'l shivered. "I just need more time."

The well bubbled and frothed, pulsing with unholy darkness.

"I will break the veil, as I promised. I sent a fool to do the task. That will not happen again."

The well bubbled and broiled, and an understanding passed from the depths into Rarnc'l's mind.

Soon I will have no need of you. Ensure you fulfil your purpose before then . . . The understanding was not anger, it was not rage or fury; it was something else. It was a pulsing, shifting feeling of the depths, like a welling emotion threatening to burst through in sobs and moans. What the demon king understood was not wrath, but crushing disappointment, and it unnerved him. It was as if the Dark was wielding the throes of apathy, pain, and anger that were but fleeting moments of joy for it. In their absence there was *nothing*. Nothing but a desire to spread its turmoil to all others.

And it would do so by any means.

Rarnc'l suppressed a sob, shook off the feeling, and backed out of the well room, slamming the door shut.

The Whim-Dark Tales continue in
"The Weight Of Joy".

A Note from the Author

Thanks for reading The Daughter Of Darkness!

Your review would make my day! An honest review on Amazon or Goodreads helps other readers find this story, and keeps me writing books for amazing readers like you.

Want more?

Continue the story in **"The Weight Of Joy"** available now!

Visit **SEANMTS.COM** to:

- **Get a free eBook (and audio stories) when you join the community newsletter**
- **Read free short stories and articles**
- **Discover more books you might love**

Stay in contact on Instagram: @seanmtshanahan

Email: sean@seanmts.com

If you enjoyed this series, you will love my other books. You can find an up to date list on my site.

Thanks again.

Take care,

Sean

About the Author

Sean M. T. Shanahan is a Science Fiction and Fantasy author from Sydney, Australia. He is known for writing emotionally gripping, high-stakes stories that blend dynamic characters with intriguing concepts and take you through darkness into the light.

He has a lifelong passion for storytelling, and since publishing his first book in 2021 has produced multiple books that span Fantasy, Steampunk, Sci-Fi, and children's fiction.

Drawing inspiration from history, science, mythology, and adventure, he weaves immersive tales that will pull you in from the start and leave you wanting more.

Besides reading and writing, Sean enjoys nature, gaming, parkour, endurance sports, and making terrible jokes.

www.ingramcontent.com/pod-product-compliance
Lightning Source LLC
Chambersburg PA
CBHW040232170726
48295CB00014B/886